BRINLIN
COVE

BOOKS BY ROBIN STEPHEN

Chronicles of the Tessilari
Tessili Academy
Tessili Rogue
Tessili Revenge

Annals of the Brinlocks
Brinlin Isle
Brinlin Forest
Brinlin Cove

Brinlin Cove

Annals of the Brinlocks: Book III

A Story of Bydaira

Robin Stephen

This is a work of fiction. All characters, events, and organization portrayed in this novel are either product's of the author's imagination or are used fictitiously.

BRINLIN COVE

Copyright © 2017 by Brown Wing Press

robinstephen.com

ISBN 978-1-946238-02-3 (ebook)
ISBN 978-1-946238-05-4 (print)

Cover design by Robin Deutschendorf
Maps by Robin Deutschendorf

Brown Wing Press
Iowa City, IA
brownwingpress.com

First Brown Wing Press Edition

This little series is dedicated to the wonderful teachers I had in 3rd, 4th, 5th, and 6th grade who went out of their way to show an interest in my youthful scribblings. It's impossible to overstate the vast impact so much early support and valuable feedback had on my desire to keep writing, and get better at it.

ELYS YINS

NELYNA
(FOG ISLES)

CARREG DINAS

GOL LEDRITH

LAN DINAS

TWO TRIALS

SERPEN

SHI

N

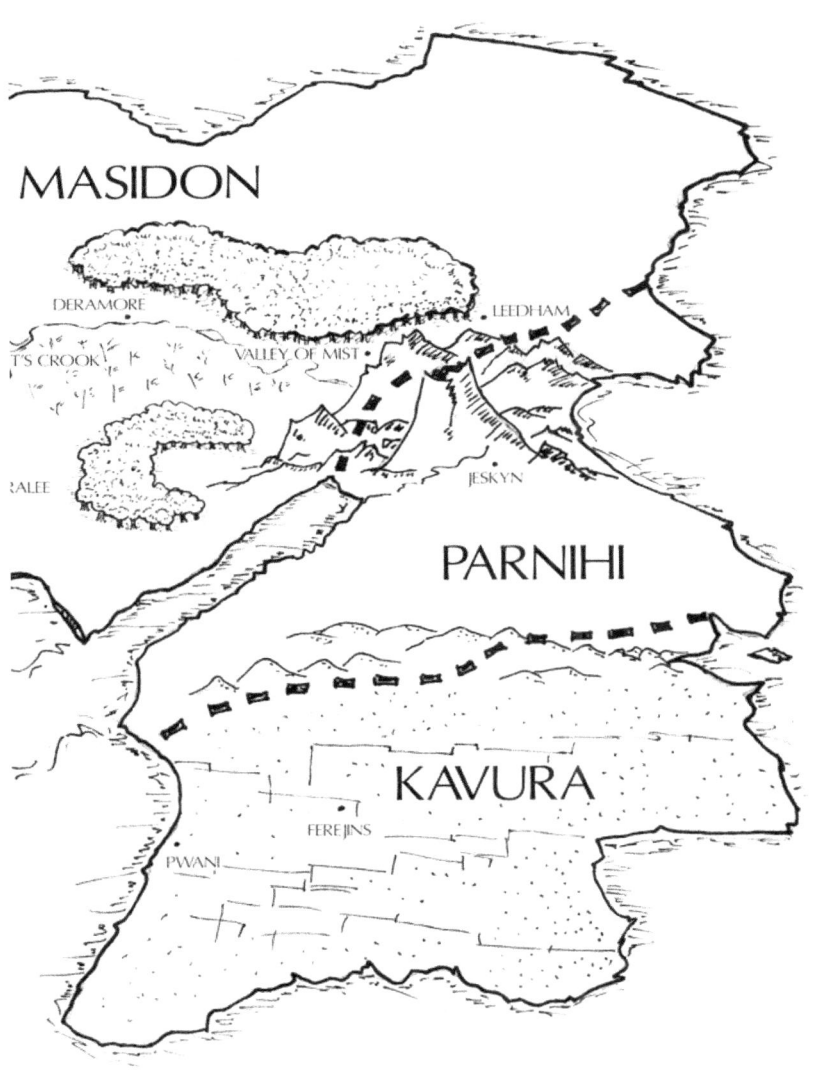

CYNNES TARTH

VAILRIA'S ISLAND

CARREG DINAS

ORB

TUNNEL

GOL LEDRITH

WARMLAKE

LAN DINAS

N

PRELUDE

Of all the things Marim feared, this moment was straight out of her nightmares.

She stood on the jagged spine of the summit of Cynnes Tarth, the fog livid and torn around her. Below her, the ancient forest was on fire. She could see the lurid glow even through the haze. Above her, the sky was murderous. Lightning raked the heavens in forks of writhing brilliance.

And she'd just watched her best friend fall to his death.

It was over. Their plan had failed. Up ahead, the massive, cracked globe that marked the summit of Cynnes Tarth flickered in and out of view with the flashing sky, spewing showers of sparks from its cracked surface. Behind her, Vailria lay as still as a corpse.

Marim wanted to rewind time, to go back five minutes and argue harder, make herself heard, make herself listened to.

It was too late. Marim felt stunned. She was shivering, but she hardly felt the cold rain. She had the vague impression someone was speaking to her, but she could not stop staring at the shifting fog, the craggy rocks up ahead.

With a sense of numb disbelief, she thought of all the steps that had led to this moment. Every link in the chain seemed so unlikely in retrospect. It seemed impossible she'd ever left Masidon in the first place, that she'd been put off her ship and left behind in Lan Dinas, that she'd stumbled upon Tassin and unlocked the secret of the Brinlocks.

Back at the academy, so many of the students had lofty goals. With the new strains of tessili seeming to manifest more and more powerful skills with each new bonding, there was excitement in every department. Long lost skills were being rediscovered, ancient magics coming alive in the world again.

Marim had never been ambitious. She'd never had any reason to think she would accomplish something grand or significant. Kix was nothing special, and neither was she. That had been clear enough from the beginning.

And yet, she always seemed to end up in these moments: these situations where she triggered something large, something terrible, something she could not contain again once it had been turned loose.

She could not go back in time and make different decisions, no matter how hard she wished to. Feeling the weight of all her mistakes mounting to an unbearable pressure, she thought how much easier it would be if she never came down from this mountain either. Surely the Brinlocks would blame her, and rightly, for this terrible storm. If anyone survived, they would demand justice.

If I die, I can't harm anybody else.

Marim took a step closer to the edge. Kix, anxious, prodded her neck with his cold, sharp nose. It was too bad she could not die without killing her tessila as well. She felt a pang for that betrayal.

Someone was speaking her name, but the idea of tumbling into oblivion was alluring in its simplicity. It filled her mind, leaving no room for any other thought, any other sensation.

It was the best way, the best thing to do.

She glanced one final time towards the cracked orb, straining to make out the uneven rocks in front of it, just in case. But he was not there. He had fallen. She'd seen him fall.

Well. He had been more talented than her by any measure. In this one thing, she could be his match.

She took another step and drew in a final breath, prepared to fling herself off the side of the mountain.

CHAPTER 1

Marim ground to a stop, panting. She could see only a few feet up the slope before the trail ahead of her was swallowed by the inevitable fog. It could be another mile to the top of the climb, for all she knew.

She tried to rally, but her legs felt like butter left out in the sun. She was hungry, too. The air up here was thin and stimulating. She'd been feeling a growl in her belly for the last hour.

Giving up, Marim flopped down on a boulder, unslung her pack from her shoulders, and called ahead. "I'm taking a break."

She situated herself on the slope. If not for the fog, she imagined she'd have a spectacular view. They'd climbed high enough this morning that the trees had changed. Instead of the towering, ancient sentinels that surrounded Gol Ledrith, these were skinny pines. The scent of their needles was a sharp snap on the wispy air.

But still, the fog. It clung to the slopes of these jagged mountains just as tenaciously as it did the fertile plains around the city of Lan Dinas, where Marim had lived for half a year after arriving here on Cynnes Tarth, the largest of the Fog Isles.

In the nine months since she'd fled the city and followed a stranger into the heart of the forest, it seemed everything had changed. For one thing, Marim was finding the fog—never her favorite feature of this place to begin with—more irritating than ever.

Settling her pack in her lap, Marim opened the leather flap and drew out the packet of cured meat and the little skin of sweet tea she'd brought with her. A moment later, she heard the scuff of light footsteps running back down the stone path. She looked up as Tassin materialized out of the mist, his faced flushed with exercise, eyes alight with the thrill of exploration. "Braven says we're almost there now."

Marim didn't move. She began to unwrap the packet of meat. "Braven's been saying that for the last two hours. I'm resting here."

Tassin stood a moment, rocking onto his toes and glancing back up the narrow trail they'd been following since dawn. He'd sprouted several inches of height since summer, and his face had taken on a new look of maturity. Looking at him, Marim felt a twinge of guilt. It was good to see him happy for once, distracted from the weight of worry he hadn't been able to put aside since the night he, Marim, and his father had fled from an angry mob.

The boy chewed his lip, eyeing the meats. "It's really true this time though. I got up above the fog myself. It happens just ahead. We were there waiting on these benches up there when we heard you say you were stopping."

Marim paused, the tantalizing spice of the meats rich in her nose. She supposed it was her own fault. She should have known better than to set out on a tough trail with Braven and Tassin for her companions. Tassin had the boundless energy of a growing child, and Braven had spent his entire life walking these forests and slopes.

With poor grace, Marim gave in. She rewrapped the meats and replaced the packet in her bag with the skin. She hauled herself to her feet and looked at Tassin, who grinned and turned to hurry back up the trail on light feet. Within moments, he'd disappeared again.

It was one of the strangest things about the fog. It could make you feel entirely alone even when there were people all around. And the problem with being alone was the way it left you with time and space to think.

Marim felt she'd spent entirely too much time thinking since she'd left Lan Dinas and come to Gol Ledrith. She thought about Embriem and what she'd done to him. She thought about the ship that was coming, bearing Coll as well as a formal delegation of Tessilari sent by the King and Queen of Masidon to make contact with the Brinlocks – the hidden race that had persisted here on this island for centuries, concealed from the world and utterly forgotten until Marim had unwittingly let the news out.

It had seemed exciting, at the time. The discovery of another people, similar to the Tessilari but different as well. It had never occurred to her not to share what she was learning about the brinlins with her contacts back at the academy. She hadn't taken time to consider the consequences. It seemed to Marim she'd done a lot of that in the last few years – setting out on a course of action without properly taking time to anticipate where it would lead.

The trail grew steeper as the pines fell away, leaving Marim feeling like she was balancing on a disembodied bit of stone surrounded on all sides by nothing but shifting, fog-filled air. A sense of vertigo swept over her. She reached out to trail her fingers along the rough stone of the slope to her right to reassure herself she was still in contact with the earth.

Then, from one step to the next, the fog grew thinner, thinner, and was gone. Marim blinked as brilliant, unfiltered sunlight fell full on her face for what seemed the first time in years. She looked ahead to see Embriem and Tassin a small distance away, seated in a kind of stone crow's nest with high-backed benches carved into the rock and a little table at its center. Braven had set out cheeses, more meats, a loaf of dark bread, and three flagons. He lifted one when he saw Marim, a grin splitting his friendly face. The young Keeper's straw-colored hair was damp and rumpled, but otherwise he appeared not at all affected by the long climb. "You made it. Hooray."

Behind the stone table and benches, Marim could see the peak of Cynnes Tarth. It reared up behind them, growing steeper and more craggy until it ended in a jagged slab of granite inscribed with runes. Carved into the rough summit sat a massive globe of stone, its surface utterly smooth except for a crack that ran through its center. The smooth sphere lay nestled as if cupped by the mountain itself, huge and looming even from this distance. Most of the runes around it were dark, but one or two glowed with a wan, feeble light.

Still a little unsteady on her feet, Marim hurried to the bench. She flopped herself onto the cool seat, setting her pack down beside her. Braven, still smiling, nudged a flagon in her direction. Marim suddenly wondered how she looked. Her face must be flushed, and she'd opened her collar an hour or two before, feeling too stifled to leave it in place. Now she buttoned it back up and made an attempt to smooth her spikey hair as Kix wheeled in from above and landed on her shoulder to strut about and hiss at Braven.

Sitting, Marim at last had a moment to take in the view, and it was every bit as astonishing as Braven had promised.

Below them lay the island of Cynnes Tarth, the details of its geography and shoreline obscured under the heavy bank of fog that hung over the land like a pale umbrella. Beyond the fog, however, the brilliant sea glittered under the sun, stretching away to meet a blank horizon on all sides but one. To the north, Marim could see the humped shapes of the other islands, each one shrouded in mist.

Braven took a sip from his flagon, his eyes brilliant as emeralds as he took in the view. "It's a good day to come. Very clear. Sometimes the fog covers the ocean, too."

They'd come up the slope from the south. Now, as she caught her breath, Marim leaned over a little, looking down the other side at the steep descent, wishing the fog would clear off so she could see what lay below. According to Braven, there was an ancient, abandoned city there, built in a sheltered cove, ringed by jagged cliffs on one side and sandy, smooth beaches on the other. It was a place he thought the ship from Masidon might be able to put in so as not to risk the hostile reception it would likely receive in Lan Dinas.

It had seemed a hopeful thing, when Braven had first mentioned the cove. Now, sitting in the sun and feeling the cool, clear air dry the sweat off her skin, Marim wasn't so sure. This would be a difficult climb to subject the Tessilari to, with any luggage they might have brought and all the different kinds of people that could be expected to attend diplomats on a mission of importance.

Marim picked up her own flagon and took a sip of the light, foamy brew the Brinlocks called tiin and drank like water though it was mildly alcoholic. Resolutely, she pulled her mind away from her troubles. They'd learn whether or not the cove would be the answer to her problem soon enough.

To distract herself, she turned again to look at the massive, rearing stone orb with its cracked surface and the runes carved around its base. "What's that?" She jutted her chin at the summit.

Braven glanced at the orb with an air of unease. "There are things like that all over the island. Leftovers from before." He shrugged and cut a sliver off one of the cheeses.

"Before what?" The tiin was going straight to Marim's head, which wasn't great considering the descent they would need to make after they ate. The last thing she needed was to break her back tumbling down some long slope. She set the flagon aside in favor of her tea.

Braven flicked invisible crumbs off his cloak as his mouth compressed into an unhappy line. Watching him, she felt a surge of gratitude for his easy-going company. She'd been among the Brinlocks for nine months now, and he was the only one who'd befriended her.

There was a long pause, as if Braven was weighing various possible responses and finding them all lacking. Finally, he looked back at her. His green eyes were grave. "Like the Tessilari, the Brinlocks sacrificed much in exchange for safety. What few secrets we have left, we keep."

✝

It had been years since Braven last made the trek over the mountain. As a boy, he'd come this way often, sometimes bringing a pack and camping out in one of the empty houses in the cove. At first, it was just a place to be alone, to withdraw from the rowdiness of the other boys and his crowded house. As he grew older, though, it became something more than that.

The elegant buildings spoke to him. The way they grew out of the very stone of the cliffs had its own silent poetry. He began to study the buildings, the way homes were connected with stone paths and bridges over canals that must have once carried water. At first, he assumed that water would have come from the sea. But after searching along the entire extent of the sandy beach, he never found a mouth of any kind. None of the canals extended so low as to come anywhere near the tide, even when it was high.

That got him thinking. The next time Braven visited the abandoned city, he came with a roll of paper and a stick of drawing coal. He began mapping the canals, tracing their origins. Gradually he discovered they all connected back to one place, combining in a great cistern that ran beneath a massive stone covered in unlit runes and disappeared beneath the mountain.

He'd dropped into the dark place beneath the boulder and walked into the dusty darkness. Dried leaves and fallen debris rustling with his every step, he'd walked back and down, back and down on an ever-descending slope until the light at the mouth was only a tiny square in the distance. So far beneath so much stone, he'd lost his nerve listening to the way his own breath echoed against the stone walls. Too spooked to go further, he'd scrambled back out into the light. Outside, he'd stood and craned his neck, looking up at the towering peak of the mountain. How deep did it go? And why was it dry?

As a teenager, he'd developed a theory. He came to believe the canals had once connected to the warmlake. Water had been pulled through the mountain and into the beautiful city so Brinlocks could live there, their brinlins free to come and go as they pleased. He could well imagine what the city must have looked like full of people, the canals alight with glittering water, stands of reeds growing in the round pools set at intervals throughout the city. He became convinced this was the solution to the overpopulation problem that had everyone so worried.

The more he thought about it, the more it made sense. Why risk populating downstream, drawing closer to the edge of the wood where they might be discovered? Why not instead re-activate the ancient canal system? As soon as they did, they'd have a pre-made city twice the size of Gol Ledrith to move into, one even more secure and isolated.

For months, Braven had haunted the abandoned city like a ghost, enchanted with his idea. He'd grown so excited, so convinced he'd uncovered a secret, he eventually requested an audience with the Wheel to explain his plan for fixing everything.

Even now, over a decade later, Braven felt a flush of embarrassment when he remembered the way he'd strode into the audience chamber and spread his crude maps on the applicant's table. He'd stood there, puffed up with the pride of his discovery, and explained how all that was needed was a crew to go into the canal tunnel and excavate a way back to the lake. Then they'd need a few talented casters to work out how to reactive the old runes that had once filled the city with water. He extrapolated at some length on his theory about how Brinlocks had made those carved stone buildings and lived there, enjoying the splendid view of the cove and the expansive beaches.

He'd stopped speaking at last, and waited for a response. During formal hearings, all the members of the Wheel sat behind screens, each within a bubble of magic that distorted the voice, making it impossible to recognize which individual member might be addressing the chamber. Braven stood with his chin raised, expecting to be praised and made much of.

Instead, a resonate voice made eerie by the distortion responded from behind a screen to his right. "The decision to abandon Carreg Dinas was not made lightly. It was done in a time of crisis. Much was sacrificed to hide us then, so we could withdraw from the world and escape the fate that befell our cousins. Shifting the shape of the island was difficult, and those who gave their strength to this work sacrificed everything to keep us, their descendants, safe. For hundreds of years, we have abided here in Gol Ledrith, and we have prospered."

There was a pause. Braven felt a dip of disbelief, felt the blood rush to his face. He had felt, all this time, the city was his somehow: its secrets unexplored. Why had it never occurred him to ask an elder about its history?

The voice continued, speaking in a slow, measured tone. "You are not the first to make this proposal. Some even on this Wheel believe the broken channel should be repaired. But I ask you, young Braven, what will happen to the houses in Gol Ledrith when the water level of the lake drops to fill those canals? Are you willing to risk the possibility we may have to abandon our homes here? How will we patrol the forest if a mountain stands between its slopes and our dwellings? And finally, what of the old, broken magic that lives even now in the mountain, calling down storms when the seasons change and causing them to linger here? Some who have studied the remnants of the old spells believe any strengthening of the flow of magic through the mountain would bring disaster down upon us in the shape of storms far worse than those we endure now."

It had gone on like that for some time. One after another, voices rose up from behind the screens, explaining all the risks of what Braven proposed to do. There was no anger in the voices, no scorn. Only the multitude of considerations he had overlooked.

When he'd been allowed to leave at last, he'd taken the maps he'd so painstakingly created and thrown them into the warmlake. Then he'd run off into the forest, half hoping he'd step on an adder just so he'd have something else to think about.

Since that day, Braven had never returned to the broken city of Carreg Dinas. But now, as he led Marim down the stone path cut into the side of the mountain, the place took his breath away as surely as it ever had in his boyhood. They descended past the stepped buildings, walking across the delicate arched bridges, gazed down into the dusty canals. He led her through the central square, where carved benches sat positioned around a large, empty pool. He tried to pretend he didn't notice the way her eyes lingered on the seats. He knew she wanted to rest. But he also knew they needed to hurry if they hoped to make it to their destination and then back over the cliffs and off the steep part of the mountain to the holding pen where they'd left the horses before the light began to fail.

He kept up a brisk walk. They shuffled through the abandoned city, three tiny figures on streets made for hundreds. They reached the seawall with the stone quay and continued on. The fog was thinner on this side of the mountain. Braven could see the white sand of the beach below, the glitter of water beyond.

Marim paused to look, but he kept going. He led her along the docks and onto the little jut of the land with a narrow path grooved into the stone. The salt was heavy on the air now, the wind from the sea a playful hand in his hair.

The trail took an upwards path that ended, at last, in a stony outcropping above the sea. Below lay the cove's mouth – a narrow channel between jagged cliffs. Braven stopped and pointed. "Here. It's the only way in. Do you think a ship could get through?" He had to raise his voice to make it carry over the crash and thunder of the surf below.

Braven knew nothing about seafaring. He'd seen ships, of course, but only from a distance. To him, they were tiny black specks that inched over the brilliant ocean like ants crawling up a boulder. Now, looking at Marim, he saw her face fall.

The mountains that encircled this cove formed almost a complete circle. They were broken only in this one place where the sea spilled in. The mouth itself was wide, but five massive spires of jagged rock jutted up out of the water at intervals, leaving only narrow channels of open water between them. There were runes on the spires, and they glowed with a quiet, pale light.

Looking at Marim, Braven could see he'd been wrong. A ship could not pass into this place. The stone spires blocked the way. And the fog seemed especially thick right around the mouth of the cove, an impenetrable bank that made it impossible to see where water ended and stone began.

They stood a moment. Braven could see the sag in Marim's shoulders. The hope that had been fueling her was spent, leaving her exhausted.

Still, she tried to rally. "Maybe they could tie up on the other side of those rocks," she said, "and row in with lifeboats."

But she didn't sound hopeful. The sea was restless here. With the fog and the chop, even Braven could see it would be a dangerous passage. One errant wave could smash a small boat against one of the stone pillars.

He felt foolish again, like he had when he'd taken his proposal to the Wheel. At least this time, it hadn't been his idea. He'd mentioned this place when Marim had asked if he knew of anywhere but Lan Dinas where a ship might land. He'd told her of the abandoned city, its silent docks. Since then, she hadn't let it drop. She'd pestered and badgered until, at last, he'd consented to bring her here.

Now, feeling the sour residue of disappointment, the three of them stood in silence, the thick, salty air rough against their faces. Tassin, standing on the edge of the outcropping, observed in a subdued voice, "Funny how they're all so evenly spaced, and so alike. The five big rocks, I mean."

Embriem looked up as a key turned in the lock, a frantic hope igniting in his chest. He sat up straighter in his padded chair, which was arranged for a view of the lake outside. He turned, straining to see who had come.

When he saw the familiar tousled head poke around the door, Embriem's hope died. The energy that had come into him for a moment drained away. He sagged back against his pillows and fixed his eyes once more on the window, no longer interested in anything.

He listened as Tassin and the grizzled man who held the keys to Embriem's prison exchanged a few sentences. The man said, "Just shout if you need anything, lad." Then came the sound of the door closing again, the latch turning.

Embriem closed his eyes. The pain, briefly obscured by hope, rose up again. Hard and sharp, it seemed to stab within his temples. Her voice echoed in the quiet reaches of his mind. *Come with me, Embriem. Now.*

But how could he go with her when he was kept locked up like a thief? It wasn't his fault he couldn't obey.

But the pain didn't care about intentions. It rewarded only action.

Tassin moved across the room on light feet. He sat down in the chair across from his father's and said hello in a tone of false cheerfulness. When Embriem made no response, his son sat in silence for a moment before continuing to speak in a dogged tone, his expression determined. "We went to the abandoned city today and saw the cove. Some of the houses are huge, and you know what? They're carved right into the cliffs and the mountainside."

Embriem opened his eyes, the bright pain shifting. "Marim? Did she go with you?" Just speaking her name gave him a little thrill of pleasure, but it also made the pain stir and come forward, shifting and stabbing.

Tassin's expression went carefully blank. He turned to look at the deepening dusk outside the window. "She'll come see you soon, father. I'm sure."

It was not wasted on Embriem that Tassin didn't answer his question. His son had developed an evasive side of his character lately that Embriem did not like. He closed his eyes again.

Giving up, Tassin rose. He walked to the trough that carried water into the room from the warmlake. In one corner, it widened out into an elevated pond where reeds grew and the water swirled in a lazy current, steam rising off the surface. "And how is Nel today?"

Embriem didn't answer. Nel was how she'd been for months – disengaged and listless, perched on a reed. Her light blue hide with its silver speckles was going scaly from lack of time spent in the water. Her eyes had a glazed look to them. Normally, a brinlin would never allow itself to be touched by any human it wasn't bound to. Now, Tassin crossed the room and gently scooped her small body into his hand.

Embriem didn't watch. He knew the routine. Tassin did this daily, at least three times, sometimes as many as five. The boy lowered his hand into the water, submerging Nel so the life-granting waters of the warmlake could replenish her energy and her hide. He scratched her under the chin, eliciting a small sound that was indicative neither of pleasure or pain. Then he reached up and broke off one of the narrow pods that grew on the reeds, cracked it open, and fed Nel one soft, buttery seed after another. She took them. Though her response was listless, she chewed them down. Tassin kept up until she turned her blunt face away and refused to continue eating.

Midway through the process, there was a disruption on the other side of the small pond. Tibs erupted out of the water, gills flared to gulp air. Embriem knew Tassin left his own brinlin far out in the warmlake each time he intended to attend to Nel, to give himself more time.

As Tibs burst out of the water, hissing and mewling with anger, Tassin spoke in a sharp, annoyed tone. "Calm down, Tibs. Sit there and wait. I'll be done in a moment."

Embriem wasn't watching, but he could imagine the sullen slink as the brilliant orange brinlin with her blue spots climbed up a reed and watched Tassin feeding Nel with smoldering, jealous eyes. No matter how many times Tassin did this, Tibs never grew easier about the process, never learned to take it in stride. Had Embriem not been too full of pain to care about anything, he might have found that interesting.

Instead, he leaned his head back against the cushions and listened to Tibs' unhappy keen until Tassin, at last, had to give in, withdraw Nel from the water and set her back on her reed. He scooped Tibs up in his hand and, without another word for his father, stalked into his own room. The boy slammed his door with unnecessary force.

Embriem drew in a breath as silence and pain combined in his system like a cruel sedative. He told himself Tassin wasn't wholly to blame for his temper. Just like Tassin and Tibs, Embriem and Nel were connected. It was, in part, his brinlin's malaise that infected Embriem, making the prospect of getting out of this chair, of caring about anything but Marim, impossible.

Outside, night continued to fall. Darkness gathered, and Embriem sat with his eyes closed. He supposed they would bring food soon, like they did twice a day, and leave it sitting by him until the gnawing hunger in his belly roused him enough to take a few bites. Still, when he heard the key in the lock again, he couldn't help but feel that spark of hope, couldn't resist turning to look.

It wasn't the stout woman who brought his meals morning and night. It wasn't he man who guarded the door. It wasn't the smooth-faced healer who prodded him with questions. And it wasn't Marim.

It was someone else entirely.

The figure that walked into the room was a tall man, much taller than Embriem, with a lean frame and hooded, colorless eyes. Quite a few Brinlocks had been to see Embriem in the months he'd been shut in this apartment, but Embriem didn't think he'd seen this one before.

He didn't care. He lay back, a feeling of exhaustion billowing through him. He closed his eyes, not even interested enough to watch as the man moved across the room and settled into the chair Tassin had vacated a short time before. He spoke in a clear, resonant tone. "Hello, Embriem. My name is Aldrath, and I am Master of Magics here in Gol Ledrith. I'd have come to you sooner, but I've been away."

Embriem did not respond. The man settled himself in the chair, smoothing his dark robes with a quiet rustle. He carried with him the spicy scent of the fog. He let a few beats pass in silence, then spoke again. "I hear you are the victim of an active persuasion spell."

This time, the words penetrated the fog of pain. The word "victim" set off a little spark of anger, and Embriem's eyes slid open of their own accord. He looked at the man, took in the deep lines of his face, the silver and green brinlin clinging just within the cowl of his robe's hood. "If you've come to help, tell that man at the door to stand aside."

A look flickered over the man's face. Regret? Annoyance? Embriem couldn't tell, didn't care. His visitor leaned back in his chair and steepled his fingers before his face. "I do hope to be able to do that one day. For now, though, I must ask you a few questions."

Solitude was not a problem for Vailria. All her life, she'd been alone. As a child, she'd been alone in her fascinations. She never liked the way other children played, so she'd played by herself.

As a teenager, she'd had a brief respite: a heady season of love and returned affection, a glimpse of a union and a future. But that hadn't lasted, and afterwards she'd been alone in her grief, alone with her terrible memories of the day her first love died. Her tragedy had set her apart from her peers, who couldn't understand what she'd lost. And it had set her apart from her elders, who seemed to believe she would recover quickly because she was young.

But what had happened that day still haunted her.

They'd been strolling along the lakeshore, holding hands. One moment he'd been perfectly fine – a straight, strong young man, full of laughter and life. She'd been in love with him, and this knowledge had made her existence both simple and happy in a way it never had been before.

Then, with no warning, her lover had pitched forward and fallen hard, collapsing onto the pebbled shore like a tossed bag of flour. She'd rolled him over, seen his blank eyes, and screamed.

She never learned what had killed his brinlin. It happened that way sometimes. Out in the lake, a fisher bird perhaps, or a predatory fish, had made an unlucky kill. There was no way to know the details.

For a long time after, Vailria had been alone because she could not abide the company of other people, couldn't bear to risk another loss. Eventually this predilection for solitude led her to train for the isolated position of a Watcher, and apply for the position outside Lan Dinas. Finally, she'd been alone in the physical sense, passing the days in her little house without company of either Brinlock or human.

Then she'd met Tommin. Young and full of dreams, he was newly arrived from one of the outer islands, and they'd been enchanted with one another from the beginning. For six months, she'd been blissfully happy. They'd spent endless hours together while his ship grew in the drydocks.

She'd known all along it was temporary. They were of an age, but he was to become a sea captain, his feet destined to spend more time on the deck of a ship than on dry land. But at least he was no Brinlock. Vailria found this comforting. He was a strong young man, and his life was linked to nothing but her. For the second time in Vailria's life, she'd been happy.

Then, Tommin had left. He'd wanted to take her with him. She'd had to explain why she could not go, entrusting him with her secret, enduring his disbelief and sadness, then watching him sail away.

He came back, though. Every time he made the dangerous crossing to and from Masidon, Tommin stopped in Lan Dinas to restock and refit his vessel, to sell the valuable goods he'd picked up on the distant continent. At least, when his ship was in port, they were together.

When Tommin returned to Lan Dinas one spring and told her of the tiny island he'd found off the tip of Cynnes Tarth, habitable but surrounded by submerged reefs and thus difficult to approach, she'd been only mildly interested. She'd listened as he described the bright white beach, the humped hills, the fertile expanse of flat land in the island's center and, most importantly, the tiny little warmlake, complete with a population of brinlins and local fog bank.

She'd asked a question or two, and he'd grown excited. This place, he told her, was their ticket to a life together. They could escape to their own private paradise. She would no longer have to live on the fringes of two cultures, keeping secrets from both. He would no longer have to risk the dangerous passage to Masidon.

He would make enough runs, stashing his profits. In a few years, he'd be able to afford timber for a house and some livestock. He'd sell the ship and its valuable guide globe, pay off his investors, and buy a light sailboat. The two of them would be free of their respective responsibilities. They could be together, be themselves, at last.

Vailria had never entirely taken the plan seriously. Even as, one visit after another, Tommin told her about his visits to the island, the way he was getting more familiar with the reef, the supply caches he was building up, the chickens he'd turned loose, in the back of her mind she'd been convinced it wouldn't happen. It had been her way of defending against hope.

But now, somehow, she was here.

Someday, Tommin assured her, they would have a proper house. It would have a deck that extended over the warmlake, with portholes in the floor and reeds in the living room, just like she wanted. Tok would never be far from her, and neither would Tommin. He'd be back in just a few weeks, with some goras and plenty of seeds for the garden and a small vessel he could manage without a crew.

That's what he'd said six months ago, anyway, when he'd left in the rowboat on his way back to the ship. She'd still been weak then, for Tok had nearly died on the journey here.

It wasn't they'd had far to come. She could see the craggy shoulders of Cynnes Tarth from the white beach Tommin had first described to her so long ago. It was the reef that surrounded this place that made the approach so treacherous. No vessel could make it through except in the calmest of seas. They'd had to wait weeks for the right conditions. The time away from a warmlake had taken its toll on Tok, and thus on her.

Now, Vailria was stronger again. But she was alone. Very, very alone.

At first, she hadn't minded. Tommin had set cornerstones for the foundation of the house. He'd left her with tools, and she'd set about doing what she could. She put in garden beds. She harvested reed stalks and wove a clumsy henhouse for the chickens. She collected reed roots and brewed tiin. And every day, she walked across the sandy beach and climbed the stone outcropping to the highest point of the island. She stared at the horizon until her eyes ached, straining for a glimpse of a vessel that was not there.

One month had passed, then another, and another. Now it was a week into the fourth month, and Vailria was growing worried. Tok was mostly recovered from the terrible depletion he'd suffered from being away from a warmlake for so long. Though he missed the brinlins he'd liked to swim with in Cynnes Tarth, he'd made some new friends now.

As his vitality renewed itself, so did Vailria's energy. The days, she found, were long. There was a little fog here, clinging over the lake, but not enough to reach much past the edge of the water. The sky was usually clear during the long months of summer, and

Vailria could watch the sun crawl its slow, slow progress across the sky.

It was in the second month she began to feel truly alone. It wasn't the lack of company that bothered her, more the realization that if something happened to Tommin, she would be stranded. No one back in Gol Ledrith knew where she'd gone. For his part, Tommin had kept this place a secret. No one would ever come looking for her here.

And that knowledge didn't lie so easy in Vailria's mind. She was used to being alone, yes, but could she really be content never seeing another human again for the rest of her life? How long would that life be if she had no company, no partner? Vailria could do many things, but building a house would be difficult without the materials Tommin had planned to bring back with him. The tent she lived in, pitched on the lakeshore, was adequate. But it would hardly offer sufficient protection again the sorts of violent storms that moved through these waters when the seasons changed.

Every day, she found herself wondering what had happened back in Gol Ledrith the night they'd fled. Had the riot spread? Were Embriem and his son safe? Or had something terrible happened?

At first, when Vailria's thoughts strayed in this direction, she told herself they deserved whatever befell them. They had rejected her advice, after all, and refused to follow her to safety when they'd had the chance.

Day by day, however, this argument rang a little more hollow in her own head. She hadn't, after all, given them a chance. She'd come in with her spells, pushing, driven by her sense of urgency. She hadn't taken time to explain, to persuade. She'd become too accustomed to her own power, too comfortable with setting her fingertips lightly on a man's arm and having him suddenly see things her way.

As the days passed and still Tommin did not return, Vailria found herself wondering if she'd made the right decision.

One morning she woke to find a chicken dead, throat torn, feathers scattered all over what she'd come to think of as her yard. After that, she set to weaving a spell into a low fence to keep anything that wasn't welcome outside its boundary. It wasn't anything formidable enough to work on a man, but it might keep the sea foxes, with their sharp teeth and slick, slinking bodies, at bay.

And finally, one day she looked out on the horizon and saw it was not empty. Squinting into the sun, she wove a small spell, cupping the air in her palm to form a looking orb.

The ship was no small craft like the one Tommin intended to bring back with him. It was a towering thing, every bit as massive as Tommin's trade vessel. Its many masts bristled like a small, floating forest, and its sails bore a crest even Vailria recognized.

She lowered her hand, feeling a strange stillness settle on her heart. In the distance, behind the ship, she could see the fog capped cliffs of Cynnes Tarth.

The Tessilari had found the Brinlocks at last.

Every morning, Marim did two things. First, she spent a moment over her stitchring, running her mind up and down the current of the magic set into the slender metal circle, adding tiny tendrils of her own energy back into the spell. It didn't need to be done daily, but it was the sort of detail one could overlook one day, and then forget about for another, and perhaps the next as well, until the spell grew ragged enough to split apart during one of its draws for the formidable power it took to transport Kix back to his brillbane bush in Tessili Academy.

Marim had a spare stitchring, and she checked that daily as well. It was the thing Professor Liam had emphasized above all others when she'd told him of her plans to travel. They'd been in his office, the large windows open and letting in the light breeze. He'd spoken in his usual quiet, certain tone as a clutch of wild tessili flew loops in the sapphire air. "Those stitchrings are your lifeline. Never forget that, Marim. Kix will die without brillbane. Outside of this valley, it does not exist. You will not have time to make it back here should those stitchrings fail. If one goes, you will be in peril. Don't waste a single day. Come back immediately."

Marim had rarely seen her mentor so serious. It made an impression, and she hadn't forgotten. She put in those minutes of effort and concentration every morning, without fail.

The second thing she did was check her tablets. She had three. The first was standard issue. Every Tessilari who graduated from the academy was given such a one, paired with a matching tablet back in the tableturie at the academy.

The second, Liam had given her as a going-away present. She'd been flattered to receive it, knowing how many students held him in high esteem and would envy her access to him.

The third was from Coll. He'd made it himself, if she could believe his story. Though she didn't doubt he had the power, she was less confident of his ability. Still, it functioned just as the others did, mirroring anything she scribed into its surface on the paired tablet he'd kept, and vice versa.

Though, honestly, he did not write to her as much as Marim would have hoped. Weeks had gone by since his last update, and it irked her. She couldn't imagine what could possibly be happening aboard the ship that was distracting enough to keep him from writing, but not important enough to tell her about.

Three days after her disappointing trek with Braven, Marim finished her maintenance work. She set one stitching back in its case and hung the other around her neck. Next, she opened a drawer in her desk and pulled out the cherry wood box that contained her tablets. As she flipped them out, she felt a small stirring of anticipation.

The first two tablets were blank. Although she'd promised both the academy and Professor Liam she would report regularly on the things she discovered about Gol Ledrith and the Brinlocks, increasingly she felt uncomfortable doing so. Time after time, she found herself sitting down and picking up the scribis, only to set it aside a moment later, having written nothing at all.

Coll's tablet she kept at the bottom, and now she expected it to look as it had been the many mornings past – smooth except for the three questions she'd sent him in the last three weeks, none of which he'd answered.

But she was wrong. There were new words on the tablet, written in Coll's slanted hand. He still hadn't answered her questions (about when they expected to arrive, what the weather was like, and who else the Tessilari had sent), but his words made her blink in surprise. "Tried to put in at Lan Dinas. Denied anchorage. Sailed around to the north of the island. Fog and cliffs make it difficult to find alternate landing site, but we are looking."

Marim's first feeling was one of annoyance. She'd told him weeks ago the Tessilari were unlikely to be allowed to dock in Lan Dinas. She'd also said she was working on finding a place for them to land. He'd apparently either ignored her or forgotten. Either was possible with Coll.

Still, she picked up her scribis and set its tip to the leather, then paused. What could she say? The wharves and docks at Carreg Dinas haunted her. Clearly, ships had once sailed into that abandoned cove. The five pillars with their runes must be a gate, made to retract below the water. If Marim could figure out how to open them, the Tessilari would have a safe haven.

She set her scribis aside, reluctant to answer Coll when she had nothing useful to tell him. Plus, maybe it would teach him a lesson if he had to wait for her to get back to him for once.

She looked about the house the Brinlocks were allowing her to stay in. It was one in a row of tidy cottages set back in the trees. It was unusual, as no flow of water pulled into it from the warmlake. Apparently, a very small number of children born in this place did not turn out to have magical talent, so a few homes existed that were equipped to house a person, but not a brinlin.

The place was simply made, but sound and comfortable. Marim was grateful to have use of it. She'd arranged her few possessions around in a way that made it feel almost like home.

Her cloak and pack were still by the door. She'd left them sitting there after her outing with Braven, too disappointed to even unpack and put things away. Now, suddenly restless, she snatched them up and hurried out into the fog.

The puzzle of the island was maddening. Or rather, what was maddening was how simple it seemed. Clearly, the Brinlocks had once lived in the beautiful city that was now abandoned. They'd once been able to open the cove, to let ships approach the docks and tie up there.

It also seemed clear whatever magic flowed through the mountain was important. She thought of the cracked globe at the summit, its few wan runes. Why had no one attempted to repair what was broken? Why leave a perfectly beautiful city uninhabited?

Leaving her house, Marim hurried to the small stable that stood not far from her house. In Masidon, horses were property, owned by individuals just like land or homes. Here, ownership of all things seemed more fluid. Anyone could borrow a horse from the stable, assuming there was one to be had.

The horses of Lan Dinas were more like ponies, really. They were small animals, both sleek and sturdy. They were bred for their trot, Braven had explained when he'd first brought her here, and could cross uneven terrain at speed without picking up a canter.

When she'd first come to this place, it had shocked her that Braven simply walked in, gave a nod to the attendant, and walked to the row of horses that stood saddled and tied to a long fence. He'd selected one for each of them. The attendant had emerged to tighten girths and help with bridling.

Now, coming alone, Marim wasn't sure she'd be granted a mount. But the same attendant was there, and Marim recognized the piebald gelding she'd ridden before. Trying to appear confident of her welcome, she walked up to the creature. He turned to her with mild curiosity and wuffed warm breath into her shirt. Feeling bold and reckless, she untied the animal and led it into the yard. The attendant watched her for a single heartbeat too long, eyes unreadable, before coming forth to help with girth and bridle just as he had the day before.

She made a few wrong turns on her way to the edge of Gol Ledrith. She was not yet familiar with all the branching streets and channels and bridges. The city was conformed to the shape of the shoreline, built out over the water in some places but not in others. There were no major streets, only curving avenues that sometimes ended in a small dock or a house built up on stilts. But the horse was sturdy and confident and didn't seem to mind running into dead ends and having to turn around. No one looked at Marim askance as she picked her way up and down streets until, at last, she found herself in a little square she recognized.

From there, it was easier. She kept at it, winding north until she eventually broke free of the city and found herself on a paved road meandering up the mountain.

Finally on her way, Marim breathed easier. The path beneath the hard, round hooves of the horse was ancient: paved with massive old stones at first, then cut into the side of the mountain itself. She let the animal set its own pace, some weight lifting off her heart as Kix wheeled in the foggy air above.

It took an hour, perhaps, to reach the place where they'd left the horses before. The path widened here, turning into a sort of paved square. Just below stood a pen, with a water trough and hay. The path continued on and up, but from here it was no longer so broad, so deliberate. It was only a narrow footpath worn into the stone through much use, too steep and slick for a mount.

Marim stopped the horse and dismounted, removing the bridle and saddle and turning the horse loose in the pen as she and Braven had done the day before. The animal ambled quietly to the water trough and drank. She then stood a moment, wondering what she was doing.

When she'd left her house that morning, she'd had no clear plan. But on her ride up from the city, she'd realized she was still thinking about the cracked globe. It sat at the summit of the mountain, and it was broken.

Marim wasn't sure what she hoped to accomplish by returning to the summit. She only wanted to see it again, she told herself, to pay closer attention to the runes around the base. How many were lit? How many were dark? She couldn't remember.

But as she latched the gate and stepped away from the horse's pen, Marim noticed the pillars. There were four of them, one set at each corner of the paved square. They were carved with runes, but the runes were dark.

She turned slowly, noting each pillar. They were thick—as thick around as three of her—but squat. The one nearest her was shorn off on one side, missing a chunk that would have been about the size of her head.

Her restless curiosity shifting to this new target, Marim walked towards the cracked pillar. Looking around on the ground, she saw a chunk of stone, rounded on one side, smooth on the top and edges. She rolled it over with her foot, revealing damp earth and a variety of scurrying insects. She brushed at the dirt adhered to the smoothed sides to reveal the carved pattern. It was unmistakably the missing piece of the pillar.

Marim stood there for a time. The fog was thin today, and wispy. It teased at her face, tracing her cheeks with cool tendrils and filling her nose with its strange spice. She could hear the chirp and flutter of birds, and the quiet snuffing and chewing of the browsing horse. She thought again of the cracked orb, Braven's answer to her question. *Like the Tessilari, we Brinlocks sacrificed much in exchange for safety.*

Safety from what? And what secret was he defending when he refused to explain about all these dead runes and broken artifacts?

Marim looked from the broken pillar to its missing piece and back again. Then, with a grunt of effort, she squatted, rocked the piece of the pillar into her arms, and stood up.

Later, Marim would never be able to explain why she did it. When pressed, she would admit she hadn't really thought it all the way through. It wasn't as if she thought she'd made an incredible discovery. There was a maintained corral right behind her, stocked with fresh hay and water. Practically everyone in Gol Ledrith must have seen these pillars. She couldn't have been the first one to notice the broken one, or see the missing chunk lying right at its base. And yet no one had done what she was doing now.

If these facts alone hadn't been clear enough, Braven's words about the cracked globe should have warned her off. But Marim was thinking only that the pillar was broken and the missing piece was right here and why not put it back where it belonged?

It wasn't easy, lifting the stone. It was heavier than expected, and awkward in her arms. She had to shift around to get a good grip. When she tried to take a step towards the pillar, the weight dragged at her. She staggered forward and thumped the chunk of stone down on the pillar's broad top. She rested a moment, then heaved at the bulky fragment until she'd rotated it into its proper position.

Once aligned, the stone wedge fit well. There were chips missing, and the sharper edges of the crack had gone soft and smooth with time. The piece she'd picked up was much darker than the rest, stained from lying among the leaves for so long. Nevertheless, it was clearly back where it belonged.

Supporting the chunk with one hand, Marim considered the pillar, the circle, and the runes. She rifled through all the spells she'd ever heard of, trying to remember if she knew one for fusing stone.

As she was thinking, she felt a strange pulse of energy under her hand. She glanced down and was surprised to see light pouring out of the crack in the stone: faint at first, but becoming brighter with every second. As she stared in consternation, the crack began to belch sparks that started off white but flared to an angry red.

Next, Marim felt a shock in her palm. With a little yelp, she leapt backwards. Rubbing her hand, she watched with dismay as light spread throughout the crack, letting off a brilliant white incandescence and filling the air with the thrum of magic.

Next to her, the mountain groaned. Pebbles tumbled down from above, and Marim felt a surge of panic. As Kix let out an eerie, nervous cry, she dove forward again. She slammed her body against the chunk of stone, trying to push it free of the pillar, to break it again.

But it was too late. The chunk was fused into place somehow, bound there by magic. Cursing uselessly, heart pounding, Marim beat at the stone with her hands, ignoring the stinging bursts of magic that shocked her every time she touched the stone.

Beside her, Kix shifted. He blurred, hissed, and suddenly materialized at a much larger size. Instead of the length of her finger, he was now the size of a large dog.

Wings beating, head raised in a defiance, Kix threw himself at the pillar, ramming into it with the compact bulk of his scaled body, clawing it with his talons. Marim had to fling herself out of his way as his rage mounted.

His fury made no impression on the pillar. The light continued to spread, bleeding out of the crack to overflow into the runes. And the sparks leapt higher, their energy bright and searing in Marim's eyes.

The light seemed to gather speed as it moved, flowing out of the one pillar into the carvings on the ground. Kix's beating wings raised a current of air, blowing away the dried leaves that lay scattered across the stone pavers. Marim could see a whole tracery of intricate carvings that lit up and began to glow.

The sparks were leaping higher than her head now. The ground was shaking beneath her feet. In its pen, the little horse released a high, nervous whinny.

Marim couldn't remove the chunk of stone. That much was obvious. What else could she do? The crack was the problem, she saw. The magic couldn't flow through the stone the way it was meant to, and so the sparks flared in the break. She needed to smooth it out, to repair the crack.

Kix was still doing battle with the pillar. Marim, overflowing with reckless determination, spoke to him. "Kix. Enough." Her tessila gave the pillar one final ineffective swipe, and slunk away. She drew on her memory. Her spellbook was in her pack, but she didn't think she had time to pull it out and read. She thought of her distant lessons at the academy, trying to remember any spell that might serve her.

Finally, she thought of one. A passive smoothing spell, usually used to join seams in fabric or leather so two parts became one. It had been a spell she could manage, though she'd never been much good at it. But she was different now. Stronger.

Squinting and grimacing, Marim stepped forward and placed her hand on the pillar. As the sparks stung her face and crackling energy flared against her palm, she wove her spell. She did it with more desperation than confidence, but the weave came easily enough. It wasn't so different from healing, she realized. There was a wound in this stone, and it needed to be smoothed over.

She could feel the sparks – alive but not hot. She could feel the trembling of the stones beneath her feet and the mountain behind her. But she remembered her lessons. She did not hurry. She closed her eyes and took the time to double-check her weave before releasing.

The spell flowed out of her, taking hold.

Silence fell. Marim opened her eyes hesitantly and looked around. The sparks were gone. The pillar beneath her hand was as smooth now as if it had never been broken. The mountain had stopped shaking.

Swallowing hard, Marim glanced back down the path. But there were no angry shouts or running footsteps. She was still alone. Maybe she could even get out of here before anyone discovered what she'd done.

A whisper of a breeze stirred the fog. Marim let out a short sigh of relief. "Delari's breath. I am a fool." She rubbed at her collar, feeling abruptly tired as her terror faded and her heart slowed its frantic pounding. She laughed. It was a shaky sound, but already she was recovering her composure. She considered the pillars as the white light within them lapsed to the quiet glow of dormant magic. "I wonder what they do."

Kix, who still hadn't entirely mastered shifting and could only make himself large when in distress, was craning his head around to admire his splendidly large wings and haunches. He was sitting on some of the runes and they added an extra luminous glow to his yellow scales. "Yes," Marim said, smiling. "You're quite impressive."

Her tessila preened, launched himself into the air, and flew up to land on a stony outcropping a few feet above Marim's head. Following his movement, she looked up.

That's when she saw the orb.

It was set into the cliff wall just below Kix's perch. It was perfectly round, and made of stone. It reminded her of the strange globe she'd seen on the summit of Cynnes Tarth. It too, was cracked down the middle. As she stood, Marim saw with a creeping horror that the light from the square was still moving, leeching up the side of the mountain to fill more traceries and runes like dye sucked up by fabric.

The orb was cracked, like the pillar had been cracked. It didn't take a genius to guess what would happen when the light reached that flawed place.

Marim's fear returned, stronger now. The globe was well above her head, too high for her to reach. Frantic, she looked for something to stand on. She thought of the horse, but it was pacing and snorting in its pen. She looked at Kix, but he wouldn't be tall enough. So she ran down to the pen, dumped the saddle onto the ground, and carried the wooden rack back up the slope with her.

Balancing on the wobbly saddlehorse, Marim could just reach the orb. The light had reached it too, by then, and white sparks were beginning to fly. But it was easier this time. Stretched and unsteady, she pressed two fingers to the stone and wove the spell with confidence. As she released, she watched the crack smooth away, disappearing in a ripple as the magic flowed out from her fingertips.

The crack sealed itself, and the sparks died, but the light continued to creep. At last, the orb glowed with a pure, unbroken luminescence. Below it, etched in that same white light, appeared the clear contours of a doorway. In the center of the door was carved a single, glowing rune.

Weak with relief, Marim stepped off her precarious perch. She carried the rack back to the shed, replaced the saddle, and returned to the outline of the door in the stone. Kix was still sitting above on his bit of stone. As she stood facing the cliff, Marim felt a terrible, creeping sensation of déjà vu. She remembered a moment long ago when she and Kix had faced almost this same situation. Except she'd been a child then, wearing a metal collar that had opened layer after layer of sores on her throat. Kix had been fastened into a weighted harness so he could not fly. They'd both been starving, terrified, and nearing the end of their stamina.

Marim blinked, remembering that terrible moment, remembering the spell Nylan had shoved into her hand, remembering the tentative weaving she'd created, released, and dropped onto the rune. She remembered how Nylan had turned on her, ready to kill her even though he'd promised he would set her and Kix free if only she did what he asked.

Her little spell had taken hold. The cliff had opened, spilling out purple darkness, and a monster.

The memories filled Marim, pulsing through her, taking over. She knew she should not do it, but the rage that had lain deep inside her since that day shifted, turning over like a sleeping dragon with a belly full of fire. She was still angry about what had happened. Angry Nylan had chosen her, angry she'd believed his lies, angry she'd been the one who released a monstrosity back on the world.

That old anger combined with the fading fear, making her reckless.

Marim didn't know much about the roots of magic, but at the academy she'd had to learn the basic runes: their names and how to weave their names as spells. The rune on this doorway was a simple one. It meant "door" or "portal" or "path," depending on the context.

Feeling an electric, heady sensation of defiance, Marim named the rune, weaving its magic as she did so. She released her spell and dropped it onto the glowing doorway.

Almost the moment the spell's energy left her, Marim felt a rush of panic. What was she doing? Hadn't she learned her lesson about opening magically sealed mountainsides? Was she trying to bring about another massacre? To cause the deaths of hundreds more people?

Already wishing she could take the spell back, Marim waited. When a moment passed and nothing happened, she let out a deep breath.

She must have gotten the weave wrong.

Then, the rumbling in the mountainside started again. The shaking began slowly, then intensified. Sheets of pebbles and sand sifted down from above. Kix, alarmed, took flight once more.

Marim's anger burned out, replaced by cold fear. She was on the point of turning, ready to charge back down to Gol Ledrith and warn the Brinlocks she'd released another monster.

But the trembling stopped as abruptly as it had begun. The door that had been only an outline split down the middle and slid to the sides, revealing a long, dimly lit tunnel that lead into the heart of the mountain.

CHAPTER 2

Braven was just setting his breakfast dishes in the basin when a pounding started on his door. Turning, he walked across his small kitchen, and answered the knock.

Outside his door, the fog was aglow with the light of morning. Marim stood on his little deck, her face was flushed as if she'd been running, her short hair disheveled, her collar askew. Her presence on his doorstep at this time of day was a small surprise, but it wasn't what caused Braven to leap backwards with a yelp and slam the door in her face.

The pounding started up again almost immediately. Braven stood for a moment with this hands against the reassuringly solid wood, trying to parse what he'd seen.

Behind Marim, perched on the railing of his deck, he'd glimpsed a massive beast covered in brilliant yellow scales. The thing had been glaring at him with angry black eyes.

He blinked several times, wondering if this was a trick. Plenty a Brinlock was talented with illusions, but Marim had told him once this was not a skill the Tessilari possessed.

Marim's voice sounded through the door. "Braven. It's just Kix. Come out. Hurry. I have to show you something."

"It's just Kix." Braven repeated the words under his breath, adding a quiet snort. Kix hated Braven. It was written in the creature's every look, every hiss, every seething reaction to Braven so much as bumping into Marim by accident. The only thing that had kept the tessila's burning dislike for him from being truly alarming was the fact that Kix was usually no larger than Gia – which was to say, too tiny to harm so much as a rabbit.

This Kix, the one Braven had glimpsed before he'd slammed the door, way plenty large to kill a rabbit. He was plenty large to kill a man, with talons and a long, muscle-bound body to make it easier.

The pounding did not cease, and Marim's voice was growing frantic. "Braven, please. It's important. It's really important."

There was a splash in the trough along the wall, and Gia appeared, leaping out of the water to climb up a reed and call to him. She was agitated, her gills flared and her wide eyes large with concern. He went to her, picked her up, and tucked her into his collar, making quiet soothing noises. Then, gathering his courage, he returned to the door and cracked it open.

Kix was still there, still perched on the railing, still glaring, still nearly the size of a gora. When he glimpsed Braven, the tessila hissed and flared his wings, revealing a wingspan fully as wide as Braven was tall.

Marim, fist still raised, turned when she heard the hiss. She saw Kix and did a double-take, then snapped out an irritated order. "Kix! That's enough. Shift back. There's no need for you to be going around like that."

The tessila hissed again. Braven considered withdrawing back inside, closing his door, and slipping out the back. He liked Marim, but not enough to risk those talons.

Marim, seeing Kix bridle at her command, stepped over to the tessila and ran a gentle hand over the brilliant yellow scales of the animal's neck. Braven felt his breath catch in his throat. The tableau they made was arresting. The girl, with her fine features and cropped hair, the tessila with his intricate wings and gleaming hide. Around them, the fog caught the light and they both seemed to incandescent.

At Marim's touch, Kix sighed, bowed his head, and disappeared. Or, at least, he seemed to disappear. What he really did was return to his diminutive size and streak off into the fog with one final, vindictive hiss.

Marim turned to Braven, face still flushed with embarrassment. "Sorry." She sounded half contrite, half amused. "I didn't realize he was managing to be so intimidating."

She led him north of the city, back the way they'd come when he'd shown her Carreg Dinas. She'd brought a mount for him and they rode at a quick trot, not speaking over the clatter of the hooves on the broad stone path. Eventually, they neared the place where the trail widened in a paved square with a short, stout pillar set at each corner.

As Marim drew her horse to a stop, Braven reined in as well. He was prepared to dismount and lead his animal down to the holding pen, but the expression on Marim's face made him stop and look around.

Braven was familiar with this place. He'd often stopped here when he was young to catch his breath and wonder at its purpose. He had long ago noted the broken pillar, the shorn off chunk lying at its base. Now, instinctively, that was where he looked.

The broken pillar was whole again, and the runes carved into its surface were alight with a mild glow. Braven stared, speechless, but before he could say anything, he became aware of a shape in the mountainside, and a strange current of cool dry air brushing his cheek.

Tearing his eyes from the pillar, Braven saw the passage. It tunneled into the mountain, wide open, looking for all the world as if it had always been there.

Braven looked to Marim, too stunned to even formulate a question. Around them, a breeze rustled the turning leaves. He could smell the fall coming – that crisp, dry beginning of things to come. Marim said, "I haven't gone in yet."

There were a million things he might have said in response. He glanced back at the repaired pillar. How many times had he looked at it as he'd walked past? How many times had he thought of setting the fallen chunk back where it belonged? But how many times had he been warned? He could hear his mother's voice, his father's, his grandfather's. "Don't touch anything carved with ancient runes. Not for an instant. Not even just once. Not ever. Promise me, Braven. Do you promise?"

Braven had promised, and every time his curiosity almost got the better of him, he imagined having to explain why he hadn't been as good as his word.

Marim was still speaking, her words tumbling out of her mouth in a rush. "I haven't gone in, but I think it leads to the cove. I think …"

He didn't wait for her to finish. He dismounted and walked away, annoyed for reasons he couldn't quite pin down. As quickly as he could, he secured the horses in the holding pen. Then, Marim at his heels, Braven strode into the mountain.

The hallway was lit by the runes carved into the stone wall, and the floor sloped gently up. Behind him, he heard Marim's soft steps. Gia shifted in his collar. She did not like enclosed places. He gave her head a little stroke, and kept walking.

He'd expected the tunnel to go all the way through the mountain, providing easy access to the abandoned city of Carreg Dinas. So it surprised him when hallways opened up abruptly, becoming a vaulted chamber with a ceiling so high he had to crane his neck up to see the peak. To his left stood one door. To his right, another. Both were closed, outlined in light, with a single rune carved into the face.

Braven stopped, turning to Marim as she hurried up behind him. "How did you open this path?" He realized his voice sounded harsh, maybe even angry. And he was a little angry. But not at Marim. Nor precisely, anyway. He was angry it had taken a stranger to come here and find something his own people never should have forgotten.

"I named the rune. I wove its spell and set it on the door."

Braven glanced at the runes on the two doors. Both were familiar to him. Marim was looking at them too. She pointed. "That one is 'tome' or 'scroll' or 'manuscript.' That one ..." she paused, forehead creased. "I don't know that one."

"It means fog. Or mist." Braven heard the edge in his voice, saw Marim shrink into herself a little. She fiddled with her collar and began to say something that sounded like an apology, but Braven spoke over her, naming the rune and weaving its sign on the air.

The stone door split down the middle and slide to the sides with an action as smooth as if it had opened just the day before. Beyond the threshold lay a room the likes of which Braven had never seen.

He stepped in, breathless. The floor was lit with traceries of magic, and more carvings crawled over the walls. The ceiling was slanted and steep, alight with pulsing lines.

In the center of the room, set into the floor, was a round table. It surface was divided into four sections by glowing lines. At the center of the table sat a large, luminous stone orb.

The room was silent, the air crisp and clean. There was no sign of dust, no stale air. The room pulsed with power, thrumming with energies Braven couldn't begin to measure or understand.

He walked forward, his soft leather shoes making no sound on the polished floor. Marim drifted after, Kix swooping in to alight on her shoulder.

They approached the table and its orb. As he drew near, Braven could see the orb's light shifting constantly. It was transparent, its interior cloudy because it was full of some kind of dense vapor.

"Fog." Marim repeated the name of the room as she stopped at the edge of the table and began to read the runes carved into its surface. There were four sections, each labeled, and the orb lay within a stone setting with an arrow carved into the lip, pointing out. Marim set her finger on the rune that labeled one section. "Lake," she said. She moved to the next. "City." She paused at the next one, uncertain. Braven named it for her. "Island." It was to this section the arrow now pointed. The last, Marim named, "Space." She paused, then amended herself. "Or, region."

Braven nodded, staring at the orb, his heart beating strangely fast. He glanced back towards the door, as if expecting someone more important to arrive, to tell them they were not welcome here. "We have to tell the Wheel about this. If this is what I think it is, it influences the amount of fog on the island. Some legends speak of this, how we used to be masters of the mist."

But Marim was looking at something else. Set into an alcove at the far end of the room was another glowing table, this one with five smooth pieces of stone standing at its center. Braven, preoccupied with the implications of the fog dial, wasn't paying enough attention. He didn't notice Marim extend her hand to touch a dial on the other table. Just when he realized she intended to change something, it was too late. With one deft movement, she rotated something. Braven heard it click into its new position.

With a little sound of dismay, he dashed around the table to see what she'd done. She looked up at him, her eyes alight with defiance as the five pillars behind her sank into the stone table. She gestured at the two runes on the lip. "Close. Open." Something in her eyes sparked. "I think the Tessilari can land now."

Cockram did not look at the man who came to his cell and opened the door. He stayed where he was, seated on his bench, eyes on the floor. The man, one of the few city guards who had retained his job after the mob rose last summer, walked in and tossed a bundle onto the bench next to him. It landed with a heavy thump. "You're free to go." He was a sturdy man, older than Cockram, his eyes the same steely gray as his hair. He said nothing more, only strode out of the cell, leaving the door open.

Cockram sat a moment longer, then reached one hand over to touch the bundle. It was a bag made of rough burlap, the weave coarse. He opened the throat and looked inside.

His belt and vest lay within, atop his shirt, long coat, and boots. All the things he'd been wearing the night he was taken into custody were now returned to his possession.

When his fingers touched the rich fabric of the shirt, he felt a slight lifting of his heart. The clothing had been laundered and folded, his boots cleaned and oiled. It was all there, down to his leather eye patch, his silken neck scarf, and his golden rooster pin.

With a sigh, Cockram heaved himself to his feet. He stepped out of the soft slippers he'd worn the last nine months. Methodically, he began to dress. Although he itched to be out of this place, although anger at what had happened still seethed in the pit of his belly, he moved with the same deliberate pace he always used to dress himself.

Nothing could be done about his rough beard. Still, as he dressed, he felt some color come back into the world, along with a little spark of excitement.

They'd taken nine months from him. For nine months, the enemy had gained ground, gained traction while Cockram sat in this cell, unable to do anything more than write his allotted two letters a week. He'd wasted one of them now and then on the cloister, but always received back the news that no new rector had yet arrived from Elys Yins and the sisters were making do as best they could. Which meant it was up to Cockram alone to prepare, to plan, to make the most of his tenuous connection to the outside world.

Tilde visited him, of course. She was as dutiful and bland as ever, sitting across from him with her hair bound up to reveal her slender throat. It seemed every time she came, she was more like her mother. The easy way she handled the guards was familiar too. She was coming into her own. She'd had nine months to develop without his guiding hand. He'd have to watch her now. He knew that.

When he was dressed, Cockram rose and settled his eyepatch over his face. He had no mirror, but nevertheless he felt a measure of peace and confidence return. It wasn't so much that he missed the eye. He found he could do without it. What he hated was the deflated eyelid, flat and formless, that destroyed the symmetry of his face.

He unbound his hair, combed it, and tied it back again. He touched the pin in his neck scarf, and felt the familiar spark of pleasure that he should own such a lovely thing. Ready at last, he strode through the open door.

The guard waited at the top of the short block of cells, most of which were empty. He was comfortably seated behind a counter, occupied with some paperwork. Cockram made as if to walk by without stopping, but the man cleared his throat. Cockram stopped, his heart giving a nervous twitch. The man extended an envelope, sealed with black wax. "Your release order, record of time served, and parole conditions."

Cockram drew in a deep breath, pushing aside the black wall of hatred that crashed over him as the man spoke. He wanted to turn on the man, to pull the club out of his belt and beat him over the head with it. He hated that this man had seen him stripped of his pride, reduced to a colorless, disfigured man in a cell. He hated that his own strength, his confidence, had been compromised to such an extent.

But attacking this man now would accomplish nothing. He was not a player. He was not a man who moved other men. He was only a cog in a machine. If Cockram took him out, he'd only be replaced by an identical moving part.

Instead of assaulting the man, Cockram turned, accepted the envelope, and tucked it inside his vest. He waited, eye fixed on the plain wooden door that led out into the guard station and Lan Dinas beyond. The guard shifted as if he intended to rise, but seemed to think better of it. He looked back down at his papers. "Don't lose those, and if we hear any report of you trying to disturb the peace again, be warned. The courts will not be so lenient a second time."

Cockram felt his expression try to twist into a sneer as his mind offered up several retorts. But he schooled his face, held his silence.

The man, annoyed now, made a curt gesture towards the door. "Now get out of here."

Cockram did. He shouldered through the door, resisting the urge to run. Moving quickly but not rushing, he strode through the outer offices and burst, at last, into the fog filled street. He drew the damp, spicy air into his lungs like a vapor drug, momentarily closing his eye.

He could smell the fog – damp and edged with the cool of dawn. He could hear the diffused bustle of the waking street – the thud of a man stacking crates onto a cart, the clatter of horse hooves on cobblestones. Cockram paused to savor his freedom for half a dozen heart beats. Then he opened his eye and turned left.

In nine months, he'd had ample time to plan his next move. There would be no mistakes this time, no more set-backs. He strode up the street with the unshakeable certainty of a man who has set his feet on a path that leads only one way.

Magics had always seemed friendly to Aldrath. He could hardly remember a time in his life when he hadn't been surrounded by them, wielded them, used them to build and nurture and develop and guide. As a boy, he'd been forever tinkering with the limits of what he could create. As a man, he'd been responsible for many of the innovations that made life in Gol Ledrith more comfortable, more convenient. He'd sat on the Wheel for a score of years now, and in that time he had mediated his share of small conflicts, many of them involving disputes over the way magics were used in day to day life.

The use of passive persuasion was forbidden between people except in cases where prescribed by the Wheel and certain rare circumstances regarding the safety and management of children. And, of course, there were exceptions for those who worked to keep Gol Ledrith safe and hidden from the wider world. That didn't mean no one ever slipped up or gave in to temptation. There were processes for dealing with the unscrupulous – steps taken to dissuade those who might be inclined to ignore the laws.

But active persuasion was something else entirely. It was a thing rarely spoken of. The fact that it was against the law hardly mattered. It had never been done in Gol Ledrith because, as far as he knew, no Brinlock could work such a casting.

But the Tessilari girl was another story. Marim had come before the Wheel when she first arrived, quiet and contrite, asking for protection and help. Although the histories warned against trusting strangers, Aldrath hadn't identified her as a threat. Now he could only hope he hadn't jeopardized his entire people by trusting her, by letting her stay.

When he'd first come to see the man Embriem, he'd done so with confidence. Never in his long life had Aldrath met a spell he couldn't master. His brinlin, Hob, was well seasoned, his magic steady and strong. But three days, now, Aldrath had come to Embriem and explored the magic Marim had set into the man, hooked into his soul like a curl of cruel wire. Three days, he'd left to meditate, certain he would come up with an answer. Three days, his thoughts did nothing but chase themselves in circles.

Now, there were reports of a ship – a massive thing with sails emblazoned with the crest of the Tessilari. It had been turned away from the docks at Lan Dinas, and now circled the island like a wolf. According to Marim, the ship bore a diplomatic delegation – a party of mages wanting to establish contact between the Brinlocks and the Tessilari. She'd asked for permission to bring them to Gol Ledrith. The Wheel, after some deliberation, had granted it. Not because any Brinlock wanted to meet the Tessilari, but because the Wheel was only too well aware that the time to hide was over. The Tessilari would come here, invited or no.

Each day, as he wrestled to free Embriem from Marim's spell, Aldrath grew more uneasy. The aggressive power of this simple weaving unnerved him, most particularly in conjunction with Marim's assertion that she had not meant to snag this man in such a way. According to her story, she'd been scared. There had been a mob about to spill into the house. Embriem had been stretch-stunned: all but debilitated by spending too much time away from his brinlin for too long. She'd meant to cast a passive persuasion spell, just to get him to go with her until they were out of danger.

It wasn't that Aldrath didn't believe her. He could see the remorse in the girl, could feel her jangling regret when she spoke of Embriem. It was the very fact that a young mage, graduated from some place she called Tessili Academy, could make such a mistake at all.

The magic and temperament of tessili, Aldrath was forced to conclude, was very different from the magic and temperament of brinlins.

Now, sitting with Embriem in the quiet apartment the Wheel had requisitioned for the man and his son to occupy, Aldrath closed his eyes. The room was quiet. Embriem's tessila, Nel, sat on a reed not far away. But she was listless, her scales dull. Embriem himself was no better. As always, he'd looked up when the door opened, hope lighting his face. But that light died as soon as he saw Aldrath.

He was in thrall to the girl. Utterly, and wholly. Even she was powerless to get him to stop following her. Before they'd locked him up here, he'd followed her constantly, seemingly without any will of his own. The man could not resist the spell, and the girl could not undo it. She he tried, and several powerful Brinlocks had tried to help her. All to no avail.

This was the problem with intuitive casting, Aldrath thought as he sat in Embriem's presence and tried to gain a new perspective on the problem. There were several schools in Gol Ledrith, some with competing views on the best way to introduce the magical arts and instill proper values and consistency in brinlings. There was even a group that advocated no schooling – of encouraging a departure from the teachings of old and letting students feel their own way to the style that worked best for them.

That was all well and good in theory. In practice, it was less romantic. Aldrath had an example of the dangers of impulsive casting sitting right in front of him.

He had some ideas, some thoughts on what he might do to help. The problem with mind magic was that it affected the psyche of the subject, and there were always risks when it came to manipulating the mind.

Now, Aldrath stirred, leaned forward, and set his hand on Embriem's arm. The man did not react.

Aldrath closed his eyes. He began to weave his spell – one that pushed out around him like a bubble. It shoved at the prickly shape of Marim's spellwork, shouldering it aside.

It was not easy, but Aldrath had not expected it to be. The further he pushed, the more resistance he encountered. Eyes closed, sweat beading on his brow, he kept up his weave until he had Embriem entirely contained within a protective shield of his own magic. Marim's magic bit and clawed at his weaving, fighting against the displacement.

Closing his mind to the pain, Aldrath opened his eyes to find Embriem staring at him with an expression of astonishment on his face. There was lucidity in his eyes, along with confusion, discomfort, and fatigue.

The other man made as if to pull his arm away from Aldrath's touch, but Aldrath tightened his grip, shook his head, and tried to explain. It was difficult to speak, to think, and to hold his spell in place against the constricting power of Marim's compulsion all at the same time. "Be still, man. We don't have much time." The words came out in a breathless gasp.

The strain was mounting by the instant, causing him far more discomfort than he'd been prepared for. Marim's magic seemed to grow bright and sharper, biting down on his mind like an iron band, fighting to return to its original shape.

Embriem stopped trying to pull away, but his body was full of tension. His eyes darted around the serene room, taking in the foggy view out the window. "Where am I?" He turned as if looking for the door. "What has happened?"

Aldrath had to struggle to clear his own thoughts enough to answer. He felt tears pooling in the corners of his eyes. "There's a spell on you. I am holding it aside, but we have only a moment. I just need to ask. What risks do you want me to take to free you? The most promising courses of treatment I can think of might backfire. They could cause permanent madness, or even death."

Already, Aldrath's weave was failing. It was snagging and snarling, coming apart in threads, collapsing back towards its center. Embriem seemed to feel it happen, and understanding came into his face. His eyes searched out Aldrath's, and held them. "Risk anything you like." His tone was hollow, voice already going dead again. "And if you cannot cure me or I lose my mind, I would sooner die than live this shadow of a life."

As the last word passed Embriem's lips, the spell collapsed. Aldrath let go of the tattered shreds with relief. As the tendrils of magic faded away on the air, all life seemed to go out of Embriem.

The man sagged back in his chair, face blank. Behind them, his brinlin gave a forlorn little cry.

Aldrath sat a moment longer, panting. He wiped his sweaty brow, uncertain how to proceed. He had Embriem's permission to take risks with the man's sanity, but Aldrath did not want to fail.

As he sat considering his next move, a rap sounded on the door. The retired Keeper who kept a watch on Embriem's door stuck his head into the room. "Aldrath, my lord, there's a man to see you. News I think you should hear."

Marim stood on the stone quay, straining to see through the fog. It had been two days since she'd opened the tunnel, and everything that had happened since had seemed to take place in a whirlwind.

Gol Ledrith was swarming like a kicked hive of the deadly ants Braven had shown her shortly after they fled Lan Dinas. Marim's discovery had turned the city on its head. She'd been called before the Wheel again, questioned more severely this time. Several of the anonymous voices had called for her to be confined, to be punished. One, in particular, had been tireless in its assertions that she was dangerous, even if she didn't mean to be. Her magics were not compatible with the way of the Brinlocks. She should be forced to leave, or be jailed.

She'd been terrified, standing in that grand domed room, listening to the distorted voices of the speakers who sat behind their luminous screens. What saved her was, ultimately, no one could prove she'd done any harm. There was even ample evidence she'd done good. The Brinlocks now had access to a fortified harbor. They could control the amount of fog on the island. There was also the not insignificant matter of the library.

Marim and Braven hadn't technically found the library. After changing the setting on the dial that controlled the harbor stones, Marim had dashed off to see if her guess had been right. The tunnel through the mountain turned out to be remarkably short and smooth. She'd hurried out the other side, through Carreg Dinas, and onto the path Braven had shown her that led out onto the tip of rock. She'd stopped above the heaving see in time to see the tips of the five massive pillars disappearing beneath the rough waves. Braven, following on her heels, had stared out into the light fog in astonishment. When he spoke, he was breathless, his tone reproachful. "Of all the rash things. What if you'd broken something? What if that hadn't worked?"

But it had worked, and no one could argue the fact afterwards. By the time she and Braven returned to the passage, other Brinlocks were there. Someone had already opened the door that stood opposite the Fog Dial's chamber. It was discovered to hold a vast, ornate library. Like the other room, the air within was crisp and cool, the tomes untouched by dust or damp or rot. Scholars had swarmed all over it within hours, and Marim had not pushed to be admitted. Reading had never been her strong point, anyway.

But she did hope they'd let Coll read some of the books. He'd been impossible to pry away from his studies even as a very small child. She could only imagine the kind of fascination a lost library would hold for him.

In the end, Marim had not been punished. But she'd been forced to make a promise. She was not to cast any spell, passive or active, that affected anything other than her tessila or her person, for as long as she remained on Cynnes Tarth.

Now, days later, Marim had no thoughts to spare for promises or secret passageways or hidden chambers or ancient manuscripts. That morning, she'd woken to find a reply on her tablet. She'd written Coll the day before, saying, "The harbor of Carreg Dinas is open and the Wheel has granted permission for the ship to come in."

He hadn't answered until the morning. Then, at last, his short response. "We land at noon."

Since the Wheel hadn't seen fit to clasp her in irons, Marim was free to meet the ship. She hadn't known who to tell, so she went alone. It was a little past noon as she stood in the weak sun, Kix wheeling in circles overhead. She considered the harbor and the wharf, wondering how the ship would land without all the men and little boats that usually helped a large vessel up to a dock.

The fog stirred, the gulls cried, and Marim waited. At last, Marim heard a shout, distorted and distant.

After that, everything happened very quickly.

The ship did not attempt to approach the quay. Instead, it dropped anchor in the center of the harbor, and sent out a rowboat. This made for the beach, forcing Marim to leave her vantage point and run down onto the sand.

It seemed to take an eternity for the small vessel to cross the glassy water of the harbor. Marim squinted into the fog, straining for details. Two figures were rowing while a third sat in the prow. Back on the deck of the ship, Marim could make out the dark shapes of moving men, busy with making the ship fast.

The rowboat approached, drawing closer with every heartbeat. Marim knew this because her heart was pounding, seeming to sound in her ears louder than the raucous cries of the sea birds and the distant crash of the surf on rock. It seemed an age since she'd seen another Tessilari. In reality, it had not even been a year.

The fog shifted around the boat, and Marim recognized the figures within. It was Coll in the prow. His sharp face was oriented in her direction, his brilliant eyes seeming to pierce the fog. Was it her imagination, or had he grown even taller since they'd parted?

Marim recognized the other two figures as well, and her mind dipped with a sense of shock. Treyam and Jey manned the oars – two of the most famous Tessilari to have ever lived. Treyam was a Peace Warden – the ultimate descendent of the most prestigious line of the ancient race. Jey was a trained assassin, the woman who had brought the old power structure in Masidon to its knees. After the War of Diodsfall, the two had married and had three children, all of whom had bonded with strong tessili and now attended the academy.

Blinking in confusion, Marim stood like a statue on the beach as the boat hit the sand and Treyam abandoned his oar to hop out into the shallows. He wore a long coat that flared around his legs. Though both his boots and his coat should have dragged through the water, the ocean drew back from him as he moved, as if understanding he was untouchable.

Jey leapt out on the other side. She did not bother with magic to keep the ocean at bay. Clad in tall boots and practical leathers, she simply strode through the water with indifference, helping Treyam haul the boat above the waterline.

Coll stayed seated in the prow until the vessel was secure. Then he stepped down onto the sand warily, as if he feared his weight might be too much for this place.

Marim, speechless, stood a short distance away. She felt locked in place by shock.

Treyam, letting go of the rope he'd used to haul the boat, reached back into the stern and pulled out an ornate, engraved staff. He straightened his coat and looked around, his eyes roving over the stepped stone houses of the abandoned city of Carreg Dinas. At last, they came to settle on Marim. She felt the twitchy urge to pull her collar higher, to make sure her scarred throat was hidden from view. She doubted Treyam knew her by sight. But he, like everyone, knew what she'd done.

If the famous Tessilari recognized her, he gave no indication. His mouth twisted in a wry smile. "Not much of a greeting party." His tone was ironic.

Marim, suddenly hot with embarrassment, hurried forward. "I'm sorry. I didn't … I mean … no one." She paused, too flustered to even look at Coll for support. She drew in a deep breath to steady herself and said in as crisp a tone as she could manage, "My contact did not mention who, exactly, would be coming."

"Why didn't you tell me?"

It was the question Marim had wanted to ask Coll for three days. It had hovered at the tip of her tongue through each formal reception, all the festive parties and civilized luncheons and formal teas various Brinlocks had thrown in an effort to make their guests feel welcome.

Jey and Treyam, as diplomatic representatives of both the King and Queen of Masidon and the Tessilari, had been given quarters in an ornate apartment at the heart of Gol Ledrith. Coll, who had no official status of any kind, had been allowed to move into the empty house next to Marim's. But none of them had spent much time in their quarters.

After she'd met them on the beach, Marim had led the tiny delegation out of Carreg Dinas. In the tunnel outside the newly discovered library, they'd come upon Aldrath, one of the Wheel. Marim knew him because he'd recently come to talk to her about Embriem. She'd hastily made introductions, and the tall man had seemed to grasp the importance of the visitors. He'd been eager, if not effusive. Soon, the three newly arrived Tessilari were being led back to Gol Ledrith by a procession of Brinlocks.

After that, the functions began. Marim's place in it all was confusing even to her. She was not privy to any exchanges Treyam and Jey might have had with the Wheel. When it came to social functions, she was always invited but never quite included. Mostly, she found herself watching events unfold from the sidelines.

It was Treyam who was in the highest demand. He seemed to have no trouble establishing a friendly rapport with anyone. He would always be standing at the center of a small crowd, smiling and laughing as his striking white tessila flew in smooth arcs above the gathered heads, the gold tips on her wings and spine making her sparkle like a tiny, brilliant star.

Jey was nearly the opposite. The tall woman with her blonde hair, dark eyes, and hardened body kept always at the edges of things, her sharp eyes wary. She replied when spoken to, but seemed to avoid conversation in favor of watching. She was the last full-fledged assassin Tessili Academy had produced before it had been reclaimed and turned into a legitimate school of magic. Although Jey had tried to distance herself from her reputation as a trained killer, Marim knew she was still considered one of the deadliest people alive.

As for Coll, he had not changed. He was never where he was supposed to be. He seemed always to strike up conversations with the most unlikely people, then disappear the moment Marim turned her back on him.

Now, at last, Marim had him cornered. A short time before, she'd seen him slip out the door at the latest party put on by one of the high families in Gol Ledrith. She'd been wandering aimlessly among chattering groups of partygoers when she saw him make his escape.

Impulsively, Marim had followed, not even pausing to take leave of the host and hostess. When she'd stepped into the streets of Gol Ledrith, she'd found the dark and quiet disorientating after the light and noise of the party. A strange, high wind was blowing through the streets, tearing the fog into tatters. She'd had to hurry to keep Coll in sight. Following, she'd felt a thrill of curiosity about where he intended to go.

But it turned out he only came back to his quarters. She'd closed the gap between them when his destination became obvious. When he turned to shut the door to his small house, she'd pushed into it, stepping across his threshold and tossing a restrained active ignition spell at a lamp on the wall all at the same time. The lamp flared to life, bathing the room in soft light.

If any of this surprised Coll, he gave no sign. He turned and hung up his cloak, saying, "Tell you what? That I wasn't the sole representative of the Tessilari come to sue for peace and friendship and free exchange of ideas? Surely you didn't think anyone at the academy would give me that kind of authority?" His tone was dismissive, but there was a hard sparkle in his eyes.

As always seemed to happen with Coll the last few years, Marim found herself on the defensive. She pulled the door shut and tried to answer him. "Of course I didn't think that." As she spoke, Coll's tessila appeared from within his collar, unwinding her sinuous body and slinking down his sleeve to fix her bright eyes on Marim. Wip was one of the new, rare variants many people had thought lost for good. Her scales were a deep, matte bronze, so dusky in certain lights as to seem frosted with smoke. "I just thought it would be, like, a clerk or something. Someone not important. If you'd have told me it was Jey and Treyam, I could have warned the Brinlocks. They'd have been more prepared."

Coll snorted again. In his languid way, he slouched across the room and began to rummage among a heap of rumpled clothing strewn untidily across a low couch. Marim felt annoyance surge through her. She was annoyed at him for always making her seem stodgy and stiff. But more than that, she was annoyed at herself for setting the wrong tone. This was the first time they'd been alone together in more than a year, and here she had them arguing.

Coll made to pull off his fine shirt and doublet. Disrupted, Wip took flight and flew about the room in a loop, then came to rest on the back of an overstuffed chair by the window. If Coll was in the least aware of Marim's eyes on his lean, bare chest, he gave no sign. He selected a black shirt from the pile, and pulled it on.

"Treyam and Jey *aren't* important. They're relics. The war they fought in is ancient history."

Marim felt her annoyance surge higher. Coll's way of dismissing any event that hadn't happened to him, personally, confounded her. How could he say such a thing, when she herself bore scars from the War of Diodsfall?

Here in the Fog Isles, Marim had almost learned to forget about her disfigurement, or at least not worry constantly about who saw the ruined skin of her neck. Now, that old prickly mix of shame and resentment rose up, bringing heat to her cheeks. She realized she'd reflexively groped for her collar, to make sure it was turned up. She forced her hands down to her side.

As Coll untied his shoes and made to step out of his trousers, Marim turned her back. Trying for an air of composure she did not feel, she walked over to the sideboard and poured herself a glass of tiin from a decanter. She was wearing a stiff dress with large skirts of a style that had been fashionable in Masidon but did not at all match the current style here, and she wished she could change into something more comfortable as well. But she didn't dare run over to her own house for fear of coming back to find Coll gone. "Don't be so dismissive. Without their fight, the risks they took, their losses, you'd have died of the hunger or been murdered in your sleep."

Coll did not react to her comment. He'd never been interested in hypotheticals or alternate versions of history. She felt a prick of longing for the boy he'd once been. He'd used to listen to her, used to look at her with admiration.

Now, as he finished changing and turned around, tying his cuffs, the young man's eyes seemed to weigh her. His focus sharpened, as if he was truly noticing her for the first time since he'd stepped out of the rowboat. "You've changed," he said. It was a simple statement of fact. His eyes flicked to Kix, who was perched on Marim's sleeve, black eyes focused on Coll's tessila. "He has, too. Normally he'd be off chasing a fly or something."

The words stung, even if they were true. Marim's cheeks felt flushed and it seemed too warm in the small room. But she could hardly fault Coll for noting the obvious. Years ago, when she'd been only a girl, she and Kix had almost died. She'd fallen in a coma for a time, but eventually woken up whole.

Kix hadn't been so lucky. His intelligence had been affected by what they'd gone through. After their ordeal, he'd been unable to focus, concentrate, or hold any thought for more than an instant. By extension, Marim's ability to wield magic had suffered.

Marim sipped the cool, frothy tiin. She tried to reorient herself. This was Coll she was talking to, not some stranger. Once, when he'd been nine, Coll had come to her in tears because some of the other boys had played a trick on him. He'd always been sensitive to any perceived slight, and he'd sobbed that night as if the world was ending. When she'd explained that sometimes people did things that were mean and said things that weren't true, he'd looked up at her with his tear streaked face and said, "You'll never lie to me, will you? Promise you won't?"

There in her ornate room in the academy, windows open to let in the warm air that carried the rich scent of brillbane, she'd given him her word. Seeming satisfied, he'd nodded, his short, dark hair rubbing against her pillow. "I'll never lie to you, either."

It had seemed a small thing at the time, but in the years that followed, he'd never let her forget the promise. Eventually, as Coll became less and less a child, it became the foundation of their strange connection.

She turned to face her oldest friend. "It's Kix," she said. "He shifted at last." She'd told him this via tablet, of course, but she could never really tell how much of their correspondence Coll absorbed.

In the dancing light of the lamps, Marim looked down at her tessila. She felt a little surge of pride. His scars—the scales that had been damaged by the weighted harness he'd fought against nearly hard enough to kill himself—were gone now, erased by the transformative healing power of shifting. If only there was such an avenue for healing her.

Coll looked at Kix a moment, then his eyes strayed from Marim to the window. He walked back across the room, retrieved his cloak from its hook, and swung it back around his shoulders. "The fog sure is annoying. Does it ever lift?"

Realizing he intended to leave, Marim gulped down the rest of the tiin and set the glass on the sideboard. Even with the buzz of the drink in her veins, she couldn't stop feeling edgy. She'd always hated the fog too, and yet hearing Coll's critical tone, she found herself arguing. "They're not called the Fog Isles for nothing, and it makes for some beautiful sunsets."

Coll gave a short laugh and reached for the doorknob. As he stepped back out into the night, Marim was hard on his heels. "Where are you going?

Outside, that strange, high wind was the only presence on the narrow street. Coll held the door as she stepped through, then secured it behind her. "To Lan Dinas. I want to see this second warmlake and the city that turned the Tessilari away."

It was not a good idea. The Brinlocks had very strict rules about who was allowed beyond the forest. They had lived within these woods for centuries, their presence never detected by the non-magical inhabitants of the island.

Now, as Coll stepped purposefully into the darkness, Marim found herself hurrying after him, her skirts a dragging weight against her legs. "Coll, no. You could get in major trouble. There's already tension and suspicion in Lan Dinas. What if you're seen? You could ruin everything."

Not even slowing, Coll looked at her dismissively. "I won't be seen," he said. And Marim knew his confidence was not misplaced. He'd been a prodigiously talented caster from the moment he'd bonded Wip.

Marim felt the flutter of panic begin to rise in her chest. With everything she'd already done to test the patience of the Brinlocks, she could not let Coll go haring off to satisfy some wild whim. Breathlessly, she tried to stop him with logic. "It's too far," she said. "Even going downstream, it's hours by boat to get to the lake, and then another hour to cross it because you have to paddle. Coming back it's even longer." She remembered the night she'd fled Lan Dinas – the endless shush and sigh of the oars dipping in and out of the water as she sat in the bottom of the boat with the terrified Tassin in her arms and Embriem wrapped in his strange, wooden silence. All that time, she'd wondered what would become of her.

Coll gave a derisive snort. "I'm not going by boat."

And indeed, he wasn't walking towards the river. He was walking away from the lights of the city, towards the woods. After a moment, he left the dirt track they'd been following and stepped off into a clearing full of tall grasses bleached silver in the moonlight. Marim, aware of the effect dew would have on her ornate slippers, stopped at its edge.

But Coll did not go much further. He proceeded to the center of the clearing and looked upward for a moment, as if assessing the surrounding trees. He then unfolded his arms. She saw he was carrying a length of rope.

All at once, she understood. Still, Wip's shift took her by surprise. One moment, Coll was a narrow, lone figure in the wind-whipped night. The next, his tessila was with him, only grown to a size so enormous, Marim reeled with pure shock at the sight.

In her time at the academy, Marim had seen tessili who could manage truly impressive scale when they shifted. Jey's tessila, Phril, was known to achieve the size of a large horse. And there were legends of a time before the fall, when some Tessilari of old had tessili that could make themselves so large they could bear the weight of a human on their back when they took to the sky.

Now, Wip was far, far larger than a horse. Staring at the hulking, shadowy shape, Marim didn't doubt the creature could carry the tall, slender boy standing beside her. As she watched, Coll made a few deft knots in his rope and secured it around Wip's shoulders. Clearly, this was something he had done before.

Panic surging through her, Marim stooped and pulled off her slippers. Leaving them lying in the road, she ran towards Coll. The grass was damp, the ground uneven. She hardly noticed. Kix, as agitated as she was, flicked and darted in the air above her. "Coll, no. Don't do this. You are risking everything. If Wip is seen by even a single person, the people of Lan Dinas will know there are Tessilari in the forest. They will come hunting, and that will mean disaster for the Brinlocks. It will mean an end to their entire way of life. They'll hate you for it. There's no way they'll let you into the library then."

Around them, the wind was a restless imp, tugging her skirts first one way, then the other. Coll was standing with one hand on the rope, ready to heave himself up Wip's shoulder and onto her back. But Marim's words appeared to have reached him. He'd stopped, and he was looking at her.

He'd always been this way – always, he would get wrapped up in an idea and he would pursue it to the end, careless of what he trampled in his quest to satisfy his own curiosity. Marim could never influence him at times like these with arguments about the greater good or human decency. Only when she could distill the consequences into something that would impact him directly could she make him reconsider.

Now, she felt the old bond of their friendship. It felt strained and thin and perhaps not up to the task. She felt the moment slipping – his desire to explore gradually overcoming the vague promise of access to a library no one had so far invited him into anyway.

Hastily, she offered him an alternative. "There are horses here," she said. "Little trotting ponies that can move at incredible speed through the trees. It's shorter to the edge of the woods from here it we go cross country than if we take the river, and Braven's shown me the trick of the misdirection spell and how to use the speedlines. The woods are full of enchantment, and actually make sure you go the way you want to go if you tap into the spells correctly. I'll show you where we can get horses, and I'll take you to the edge of the forest. You can see Lan Dinas from there, but we won't be close enough to risk being seen."

Her words hung between them, thin and pale on the breeze. She wasn't being entirely honest. You could see Lan Dinas from the edge of the woods, but only a few outlying huts in the distance. Also, it would take them over an hour to get there, even with the fast trotting horses and the magic. Her secret hope was Coll would tire of the scheme before they got too far into it.

In the end, it was Wip who made the decision. While Coll was still making up his mind, the hulking tessila disappeared. One moment, she was a massive beast, her wings rising high towards the tops of the trees. Then, without warning, she shrank and became nothing more than a flitting speck on the night air.

The rope, empty, fell to the ground. Coll stooped to retrieve it. He looked at Marim with a shrug and admitted mildly, "She doesn't really like carrying me."

Marim had expected Coll to be impatient with her request to change clothes, but his mood seemed to have undergone one of its characteristic shifts. He waited in her front room while she retreated into her narrow bedchamber and scrambled out of her dress and into the plain, serviceable garments she wore to hike and ride. She emerged, flustered and breathless, convinced he'd have slipped out, to find him standing quietly in the front room. Soon, she was leading him out into the night again, where they found horses waiting in the holding pen like usual, dozing as they stood tied.

It was not the same attendant that helped them into bridles, and Marim didn't recognize any of the horses either. There were also far fewer of them at ready than on her previous visits. Marim supposed there was less need for the animals at night.

The attendant took their names for the log, but otherwise didn't seem to wonder why two of the visiting Tessilari were riding off into the darkness. Perhaps the man didn't recognize them. He seemed sleepy and disinterested, keen to return to his little hut with his lamp and a glass of tiin.

Soon enough, Marim and Coll were riding steadily away from Gol Ledrith, pushing the lean, sturdy horses into their rapid, pacing trot. Marim explained to Coll about the spell on the woods, and the little threads of magic woven between certain trees that, when followed, made you travel faster without expending any additional effort. These were the secrets of how the Brinlocks could move through the woods so freely and easily while anyone from Lan Dinas would wander and stumble and sometimes never find their way out.

It was pleasant to ride among the great trees in the silvery moonlight. Long ago, when he'd been a child, Marim had often explained things to Coll. It felt comfortable, now, to resume that roll. She led him with confidence, feeling the odd rushing boost of the magic that surrounded them. Marim felt her anxiety begin to bleed away. This was ok, she told herself. As long as they didn't approach Lan Dinas, they weren't breaking any rules.

She'd just begun to explain about Brinlocks and brinlins and the differences in the magics they could wield when she felt a strange thrum on the air. Behind her, Coll reined in so abruptly his horse tossed its head and snorted. Marim followed suit, but more gently, and turned in her saddle to see Coll sitting stock still, his face raised into the wind like a scenting hound.

Marim waited, holding her breath. One beat later, she felt it again – a strange thrumming note of magic. It reached them and seemed to hang on the air for a heartbeat before falling apart.

Uncertain, she looked back to Coll. He was staring into the distance, eyes intent. "What was that?" she asked.

"Didn't you hear?" Coll was already nudging his horse forward again, moving out of his place behind her and pushing the animal into the lead. "Someone's calling for help."

Then, the pulse came a third time. Marim, focused now, caught the word within the magic. She seemed to feel it in her very bones, and she recognized the familiar feel of the magic. *Help.*

She gasped. "Braven," she said. "He's on patrol tonight."

Interest flared into Coll's face. As the pulse came a fourth time, he reached up with a hand, flinging a quick weaving around the fading magic. He caught the magic before it could fall to pieces, and a luminous line appeared in the air, leading them further into the woods.

CHAPTER 3

Braven didn't usually work the night patrol. He preferred to be outside in the morning. He liked to come on shift just before sunrise, so he was beneath the great trees as the sky paled with dawn and slow sunbeams filtered through the fog to illuminate the leaves.

During the day, the forest was divided into thirty patrols. Each Brinlock monitored one sector. He rode his perimeter at the beginning of his shift, setting down the lines of spellwork that would alert him if someone came into his territory. Then it was mostly a question of either wandering about or sitting and waiting for time to pass. Few people came into the forest. Generations of Brinlocks had done their job well.

At night, there were only ten patrols, and each Brinlock covered a much larger region. At night, one was far more likely to meet a dire beneath the great trees than another human. Although the woods were not as dangerous as the people of Lan Dinas thought, there was still plenty of peril beneath the ancient trees.

Braven was working the night shift because he'd asked a friend to trade patrols with him. The friend was a young woman who looked up to Braven and didn't have the seniority for preferred slots. She'd been delighted to change with him, as it meant she could attend the grand party being thrown that night in honor of the Tessilari – the very event Braven wanted to miss.

It wasn't that Braven didn't like Tessilari in general. He'd grown fond of Marim. He found her interesting and fun and cute. But he didn't like the other one – the tall, sulky teenager Marim had introduced as Coll. He didn't like the boy's attitude or demeanor, and he didn't like his tessila. Most of all, he didn't like the way he looked at Marim, or the subtle shifts he'd noticed in the way she behaved since her friend's arrival.

A better man would have confronted the situation. Braven did the opposite. Having procured the night shift, he rode into the woods as the sun was setting, absolved of any obligation to attend a party where he would have to watch Marim watch her friend while he ignored her.

He used the speedlines and speedy trot of his mount to reach his sector, set down his perimeter magic, and retreated to a small vale, silver with moonlight. There, he removed his horse's bridle so the animal could browse, and settled onto the soft ground near a giant fern. He pulled his lute off his back, but only held it in his arms for a long time. He felt no desire to sing or strum. Eventually, he set it aside.

He should be angry with Marim. Many of the Brinlocks were. First, she'd set an active persuasion spell into a man and left it there, effectively stealing his free will. Then she'd interfered with ancient artifacts, showing no apparent understanding of the risk she'd taken. Finally, she'd revealed the existence of Gol Ledrith to the Tessilari. It was the disaster his people had guarded against for centuries.

Braven should have been furious with her for these transgressions, and he should be wracked with remorse and shame for his part in the events that had caused such change. After all, he was the one who had led Marim to Gol Ledrith.

Yet, somehow, Braven regretted nothing. The fog dial was exciting, the harbor gate was revolutionary, and who knew what secrets the library might hold? Braven couldn't help but wonder why it had taken an outsider to reveal what anyone with an observant eye and the teeniest bit of curiosity might have uncovered ages ago.

It was fear, of course. The Brinlocks were afraid. Their entire culture, lifestyle, and environment was built around that fear. But it was a fear founded in hypotheticals, centered on running from things that *might* happen. The changes Marim had forced were what his people needed. There was no escaping the world now, and everyone would see it wasn't so bad.

At least, this was what he hoped. He sat back against his tree as the moon made her slow way across the sky. He understood the mindset. It was easy to stare into the darkness and see danger.

Once, he was all but certain he saw a dire – a lean form slinking behind a spray of fern leaves that turned out only to be a branch caught in a slight breeze. Another time, he could have sworn he felt the tiny stamp of swarming ants on his fingers. He'd snatched his hand up to find nothing on it all.

So when he first saw the shimmer of torchlight in the trees, Braven didn't immediately believe what he saw. He caught a glimpse of the odd luminance in the sky and stared, trying to understand. He was still seated, still immobile, when he felt his trip line snap. His spell, broken, sang back to him, bringing with it a sharp sting.

Startled, Braven leapt to his feet. Within a moment, he was striding towards the light. His sector, the one he'd borrowed from his friend, was long and narrow, covering a portion of the edge of the wood and stretching deeper back towards Gol Ledrith. Most activity, of course, happened near the wood's edge, so that was where he'd positioned himself to wait. So he only passed a few trees before he saw them.

There was a group of men in the woods. They were not Brinlocks. They carried burning torches that gave off sharp, tarry smoke. Worse, Braven saw the glint of torchlight on metal. There were at least a dozen men, and every single one carried an axe.

As Braven crept closer on silent feet, one man positioned himself before the others and began to speak. Braven didn't catch what he was saying at first, but as he drew near he heard the man give his order. "Now spread out, all of you. Pick a tree, one each, or double or triple up on the big ones. Wait for my word."

Braven felt the world tip sideways. Horror gripped him. He caught onto a nearby trunk to steady himself. As the men moved off, alone or in small clusters, his eyes darted frantically among them. There were too many of them, and this was happening too fast. Nothing in all his history of patrolling the woods had prepared him for this.

The men did as they were told. Some moved with confidence, others with uncertainty. But gradually they spread out, positioning themselves in front of the various trees, and waited.

Time seemed to have bolted. Braven needed to act, to call for help, to stop these men. He needed to come up with some means to drive them away, or at least slow them down. But his mind seemed paralyzed with the enormity of what was happening and the memory of the other time he'd seen a man with an axe in these woods. His angry weave, that slip, and then the terrible groan and the blood.

According to Adni, that man had died.

Stunned and horrified, Braven only watched.

The leader of the men was the only one who did not carry an axe. He stood at the center of the group, arms crossed across his broad chest. In the leaping shadows, there was something odd about his face. He was wearing an eye patch.

"Plant your torches." The man's voice was a bellow on the silver air. The men, one by one, made stabbing gestures towards the ground. Braven saw the torches they carried were mounted to sharpened sticks so they could be driven into the soil.

"Now," the man with the eyepatch said, "on my mark."

Braven's heart was pounding so hard he could feel it shaking his teeth. This *couldn't* be happening. One man with an axe had been bad enough. He'd killed that man, and that should have been the end of it. Now there were a dozen men here. No, a score. And Braven was alone. Gia wasn't even with him. She was back at the warmlake, and Braven had no time.

Frantic and furious, Braven improvised. He sent out a pulse of magic, infusing it with one word. "Help."

He wove the spell, released, and felt the power slither away from him, drawn back towards the warmlake from whence it had come. He waited a few heartbeats, sent the pulse again, again, then one more time.

Then, there was no more time. As the man began to count down from three, Braven crept towards the torches. As he moved, he began to weave. One by one, a pack of dires appeared around him, lean, with fierce flat eyes.

Braven might not be able to harm these men, but maybe he could scare them off.

꘏

Marim's horse was moving far too fast, careening at a headlong pace in pursuit of Coll's. Coll rode his without fear or restraint, urging his own animal faster and faster. The creature seemed to fly as its legs extended and the staccato of its strange, two-beat pace filled the woods. Marim, too aware of the dips and gullies and stones hidden within stands of ferns, at last reined her own horse in.

Coll noticed the widening gap between them. Realizing he was going to leave her behind, he turned and tossed a spell into the air. Marim caught it, nearly fumbled the weave, and then made her grip fast. A luminous line appeared between the two of them, like the one Coll was following to Braven. Then, Coll was gone, his horse flashing around the trunk of a massive tree and disappearing into the silver night.

It was the better plan. Marim had never been particularly athletic, and though all students at the academy learned to ride, she hadn't reveled in the horses as some of her peers had. She and Coll had ridden together sometimes, but even as a boy he'd found her too conservative to be a good companion.

Marim's horse tossed its head against her restraining hands a time or two, not wanting to be left behind. But finally the animal settled into a slower version of its strange trot. The night seeming suddenly vast and silent around them, Marim rode on, following the sliver of magic that would take her to Coll.

She wondered as she rode if anyone else had heard Braven's call. Surely, Braven wasn't the only Brinlock patrolling tonight. Surely, she and Coll wouldn't be the only help that came.

Marim's horse trotted down one side of a steep hill as Marim wiped sweat from her forehead, straining her ears for any sound. The fog was thin beneath the trees, but luminous with the light of the moon. Kix, who'd been clinging to her collar, now darted up to dance on the air above her, the yellow of his scales bleached to white. Whatever had happened to Braven, she reassured herself, Coll would be more than able to help with. Possibly, nothing was really even wrong at all. They'd all have a grand laugh at the misunderstanding when they found Braven and discovered everything was fine.

She'd almost convinced herself she and Coll had overreacted when she heard the first scream. "Delari's breath," she cursed, and urged her horse back into a faster trot. At the same moment, Coll dropped his end of the guiding spell. The tread of magic that had been showing her the way unraveled, and disappeared.

For a moment, Marim felt as unmoored as a ship in a storm. But then the horse passed a trunk, and she saw a flare of light ahead. She reined in and stared. There were flickers of movement between the trees ahead. She guided her horse down a short slope, up the other side, and then pulled the animal to a halt.

The scene before Marim was pure chaos. There were men everywhere, and they were not Brinlocks. The light came from the stabbing flames of torches that threw lurid shadows among the trunks. The air was full of the babble of voices and cries of fear, and Marim saw why.

Among the men, there were dires. The great predatory animals seemed to be everywhere, prowling, slinking, creeping around trees to jump out at men, snapping and growling, their long teeth flashing in the moonlight. They were menacing the men, but they weren't actually attacking.

It took only a heartbeat for Marim to understand. The dires were not real. They were only illusions, called up by Braven to try to defend the forest.

Realizing this, Marim understood for the first time how vulnerable the Brinlocks really were. She sat in her saddle as her horse tossed its head, snorted, and tried to turn around. As she wrestled it back around, a sound registered on her ears. It was far worse than the snarling and snapping of dires, or the cries and shouts of men. She felt a shudder run through her as she registered the rhythmic crack of axes biting into trees.

All the men, she realized, carried axes. Some were using them to hold dires at bay, while others were energetically chopping at the trees.

Marim felt abruptly ill. This was an attack: a full scale assault on the forest. As she urged her balky horse forward, she heard a voice, vaguely familiar, booming through the trees. "Ignore the dires. They can't hurt you. Focus on the trees."

Trying to make sense of the chaos, Marim swept the nearby trees for signs of her friends. She saw Coll's horse standing in hobbles and looking nervous, its reins tied back to its saddle. She hurried over to it, dismounted, and hobbled her mount as well.

Her horse attended to, Marim took a few steps towards the chaos. At last, she caught sight of Braven. He stood behind a large tree, Coll right next to him. They appeared to be arguing. Marim jogged up to them, and she could see the strain on Braven's face. She could hardly believe he could talk and hold so many illusions in existence at once.

As she walked up, she caught the end of what he was saying. "When they die, it only makes things worse." His voice was strained, and there were beads of sweat standing out on his brow.

Marim glanced towards the men, the crack crack of the axes filling her ears. How much damage had they done already? Coll, following her gaze, seemed to be thinking the same thing.

Looking at her old friend, Marim felt a frisson of unease. She recognized the set in his jaw and shoulders. Worse, she saw a spark in his eyes – something wild and bright she had seen there before. He answered Braven with scorn. "I thought your people held these trees sacred. I thought your entire way of life revolved around keeping the islanders out of these woods." He made a gesture towards the lurid torches, and his words were punctuated by the relentless staccato of the busy axes.

Braven wiped his forehead and glanced behind him, as if hoping better help would arrive. He then turned his attention once more towards the men, implicitly dismissing Coll. "This isn't your battle, Tessilari. Help me with my illusions, or go home."

The worst thing to do when Coll was in one of these moods, Marim knew, was fail to take him seriously. She took a step forward, reaching out her hand as if she could somehow stop what was about to happen.

But it was already too late. Coll stepped away from Braven, and his reply dripped with scorn. "Tessilari don't deal in illusions, mistboy. We deal in blood."

With that, Coll stepped out from behind a tree and strode straight into the chaos of torchlight, axes, and dires.

Later, when she thought back on what happened next, Marim would always feel a strange shiver that was equal parts admiration and horror. There could be no denying what Coll did that night represented a display of power unseen in modern times. The magic Coll called up as she and Braven watched was reminiscent of legends – the stuff of histories and the Tessilari of old.

First, he called to Wip. She came, a tiny shard of shadow in the darkness, circled him once, and flashed away. For an instant, Marim lost sight of her, and all was still except for the terrible beat of the axes.

Then, there was a bellow. Wip was diminutive no longer. She had shifted once more, and become a massive thing – a long, coiled body, seemingly black in the dancing shadows.

She materialized next to one man who stood before a tree with a large chunk already hacked out of its trunk. He stood with an expression of intensity on his face, feet planted, axe raised. He didn't even have time to see the tessila before she swiped at him with the talons of one massive forepaw. He cried out as he was flung away, the axe spinning free of his hands. His body made a smooth arc in the air, then smashed against the trunk of a tree and slid to the ground.

In the dark, the view broken up by dark trunks and shadows, it took the other men a moment to realize what was happening. By then, the massive Wip had taken out three more men – one with her snapping jaws, one with her other forepaw, and the last with her lashing tail. As the shouts devolved into screams and men began to break and run, Coll strode into the thick of it and slammed his staff into the ground.

A ripple of pure force went out from the point where his staff met the earth, expanding in an ever widening ring. As it reached the surrounding men, it caught onto them and held, arresting them where they stood. Marim felt it pass over her, felt it snatch and grab at her feet. With a surge of fear, she blasted at it with an active strike spell. The weaving fell away.

Then she looked at Braven. The Brinlock's eyes were wild, his legs giving strange twitches as if he was trying to lift his boots but they'd grown too heavy. "Marim," Braven gasped. His voice was full of fear. In the distance, his illusions, so convincing a moment before, blinked out of existence.

Annoyed at Coll for failing to target only his enemies, Marim fired off another active strike spell, freeing Braven as well.

But the men among the trees were not so lucky. Coll stood, his face bathed in torchlight, his staff set firmly on the ground, as the men around him stood stuck in place. Wip, enraged and massive, barreled from one to the next, leaving carnage in her wake.

Marim watched as Wip tore one man in two with her talons, and snapped another's back with a flick of her tail. At last, she looked aside, too sickened to watch any longer. A few feet away, Braven dropped to his knees and vomited onto a fern.

The forest was alive with evil. All around, men screamed and died. Cockram could feel the magic gripping his feet, holding him in place. In the distance, he could hear the rampaging monster.

Panic swallowed him whole. He remembered another night, over a year ago now, when a creature had flown out of the darkness and destroyed his eye. He'd thought himself lost then, but he'd survived. He'd learned to live with his deformity. He'd battled on. The night of the riots, when the Tessilari girl disappeared, he'd thought she'd made it onto the ship after all, or found another way off the island.

Now, he knew better. The bellows and crashes of a monster in the darkness were all too familiar. He recognized the signs. In the flickering torchlight, he could see her abominable companion, blown up to thousands of times it usual size. As Cockram watched helplessly, it killed. It descended on one immobilized man after another, leaving corpses strewn across the forest floor.

Cockram struggled, fighting the magic that held him. He could hardly believe just a handful of days ago, he'd been walking out of the jail. That day, he'd gone home, greeted his daughter, and had a shave. Then he'd gone out to meet the men he'd been corresponding with the many months he spent behind bars. What he'd learned that first night of his freedom had warmed his heart. Although he'd been arrested for disturbing the peace, although many people in Lan Dinas now muttered when they saw him, pointed fingers and made accusations behind his back, a small number of elite men had seen the truth in Cockram's crusade. These men had banded together when he'd been locked up. They'd worked to prepare themselves for his eventual release, following his instructions, stockpiling supplies, and setting everything in motion. All Cockram had needed to do was step in and lead his men to their victory.

Only now, it seemed the only thing Cockram had led these men to was their annihilation. In the light of the moon and the torches, he could scarcely keep track of the shadow that was the deadly tessila. He could only hear screams and moans and other sounds, too terrible even to register.

In all the time he'd been in prison, Cockram had tried not to think about what had happened that night outside of Embriem's house. He was certain now he'd not really faced his sister. The Tessilari girl must have infiltrated his mind, called upon his most painful memories and summoned the ghost that would hurt him most. She'd deployed his most well-guarded secret against him.

What had happened, the power he'd used to defend himself, must have been a trick as well. There was no other explanation. No man could wield magic, not without first sacrificing his soul and binding himself to an abomination. Yet somehow, in the darkness and the fog, Cockram had. The crowd had seen it.

He'd managed to divert attention away from what he'd done. First, the crowd's, then his own.

Now, though, as Cockram stood in the shadow of a tree and awaited his death, he began to wonder. Magic held him. He could feel its grip on his legs. No matter how he struggled, he could not break free. He was bound up in it, held fast. All around him, men who had come to the wood tonight certain they'd emerge victorious and wealthy, dragging logs that would produce enough timber to see them all out of their little shacks and into houses on high street, died and died.

This wasn't how it was supposed to happen. Everyone had agreed the problem with the woods was that everyone was so afraid of them. Men went in alone, creeping and vulnerable. What was needed was a group – a show of force. Cockram had seen it all so clearly. When he'd led his men past the first trees tonight, he'd felt nothing but confidence. And for a time he'd stood among them, the blood surging in his veins as he listened to the glorious sound of the chopping – that rhythmic, resonant beat that signified progress.

Only it hadn't lasted. Not a single tree had been felled, but men were being taken down aplenty.

A short distance away, Cockram could see a man who had fallen to his knees and now knelt upon the loamy ground, hands held out in supplication. As Cockram watched, a massive, scaled head descended, maw gaping, eyes pitiless. The creature struck once, temporarily blocking the man from Cockram's view. When it withdrew, the man's body, headless, toppled slowly to the ground.

It was too much. Fear boiled up in Cockram, sharp and vile and urgent. He closed his eyes, reached into that place he'd accessed only once before. At the same time, he raised his hand, groping for his lapel. He felt the sparking presence of his rooster pin.

Not knowing how he did it, Cockram found power within himself. He didn't stop to think, didn't hesitate or wonder. Using the bright presence of the pin to focus his own power, he lashed out at the gripping bonds that held him in place. Blue fire danced up around his legs, lurid and luminous amidst the dark trunks.

The magic that held him fought back for an instant, then fell away.

Cockram didn't wait to see if anyone had seen the light. He simply ran. As he pelted away from the scene of the carnage, he heard the voice of the Tessilari girl, heard it clearly as she screamed, "Coll, that's enough! These men are not fighting. They have dropped their axes. They are beaten. We are not murderers, and you will stop this. Now."

The forest had gone quiet, but the stillness was almost as bad as the previous cacophony had been. Marim moved among the guttering torches and fallen axes in a suspended space of horror-filled disbelief. Many trees had been injured. She approached the one with the most damage. It was a massive specimen, with a broad, well-shaped trunk out of which a wedge the size of her head had been chopped. The sight made her wince. She could feel the tree's pain, dark on the air, and somehow sad.

All around, the forest seemed to be holding its breath. Coll was a dark statue standing in the center of the carnage Wip had wrought. Wip, for her part, was tiny again, docile and seemingly harmless, retreating into Coll's collar to sleep off her binge of violence.

Kix was agitated. He clung to Marim's sleeve, looking around the forest with worried eyes. Braven was gone. He'd run back to Gol Ledrith for healers.

Marim knew it was already too late for the men who'd been torn apart by Wip. And, if she was being honest, she felt only a passing pity for them. The trees in this forest were centuries old. They were old and stately and vital. To chop one down was a folly. It was a waste. It was an act of hubris, a short-sighted, wanton attack on the natural world.

These men had come to the forest with violent intentions. Their actions had declared war.

Still, while she couldn't condone what the men had done, Coll's response struck her as excessive. Her attempted intervention hadn't saved a single life. Wip had not stopped until there were no men left. She wondered how many had died, but had no stomach for counting bodies.

The trees needed her, anyway. She approached the one with its missing chunk and set her hands on the weathered bark. She closed her eyes as Kix perched on her shoulder, wings flared as if he thought he might need to take flight at any moment. His agitated emotions were a tug on her concentration.

She soothed him, murmuring in a low voice, reminding him of her love for him, their shared power. They knew Coll. He was no threat to them. As she kept up her flow of soothing emotion, Kix grudgingly calmed. At last, her tessila folded his wings and climbed into her collar to press his soft, cool body against the marred skin of her throat.

Marim had never tried to heal a plant before, though in her years at the academy she'd tried to cure all manners of illness she encountered in animals and humans alike. Secretly, she suspected her dedication to the healing arts was the only reason the academy had allowed her to graduate. And even with all her work and effort, she had never been a powerful healer. What she'd been was persistent. She'd been so weak then, her bond with Kix so muddled, her approach had always focused on helping the body to help itself. She'd watched stronger healers simply call up the power to seal over a wound or knit a bone back together. Such feats had been beyond her.

Back then, Marim had watched such workings with helpless envy. She knew the theory, of course. But theory without power was as useless as desire without action.

Now, it took a while for Marim to align herself with the tree. Its metabolism was alien to her, the feel of its life force stately and steady and alive with pain.

While she stood with the tree, Marim was aware of the sounds of the forest, aware of Coll still standing nearby, his quick breathing slowing down by degrees. It was hard not to be distracted by wondering what he was thinking. Did he feel proud of what he'd done? Or was he sickened to look upon the bodies of those he had killed?

In the distance, Marim heard the soft hoof beats of approaching horses. They came from within the forest, many horses moving at a fast trot. It was the Brinlocks. Some others must have heard Braven's cry after all.

She heard Coll move, walking towards the sounds of approach. For one sliver an instant, she felt a prick of fear. What if he turned his magic against the Brinlocks next, loosed Wip again in all her terrible fury?

But no. That was madness. Coll had done what he'd done to defend the Brinlocks. And it *had* been necessary. If the people from Lan Dinas succeeded in chopping down even one tree, the story of these woods would change. For centuries, the Brinlocks had defended the forest with legends, illusions, and mind games. That kind of defense would not hold up against the cold reality of an axe chopping through an ancient trunk.

With a shiver, Marim remembered the look in Braven's eyes when Coll's magic had grabbed hold of him. He'd been unable to strike at it, unable to fight. He'd been as helpless as the men out there who'd died. Not that Wip would have attacked Braven, of course. But Marim was beginning to understand why the Brinlocks had worked so hard to stay hidden.

She thought back to her time living in Embriem's house, the spells Tassin had found easy and the one's he'd been unable to even begin to grasp. She'd suspected then that the tone and timber of Brinlin magic was different, but she hadn't realized exactly what that meant.

She thought of the illusion of dires Braven had called up. They'd been perfect – works of art, moving among the trees, catching light and shadow, entirely convincing. Vailria could summon and hold illusions as well. It was how they'd spirited Tassin away from imminent death.

Marim couldn't even begin to guess at how a person might create an illusion. It felt as impossible to her as the thought of trying to fly. In all her time at the academy, she'd never heard of anyone creating illusions.

Braven could summon an entire pack of dires, but he could not break free of Coll's grasping magic.

The horses drew closer. Marim kept her eyes closed and forced her thoughts deeper into the tree. Whatever was going to play about between Coll and the Brinlocks, it would not help her to get in the middle. She heard voices, a number of gasps and muttered curses as the approaching party caught sight of the carnage.

Healing magic was quiet and gentle – the work of peace. Marim drew away from the world, plunging herself into the tree. She felt the grain in the ancient wood, felt the broken, ragged ends of the wound in its hard flesh. She drew on Kix's power. *There is so much of it now.* She focused, and forgot about everything but this one break in the world – something she could fix.

She began to weave. For a moment, she was overcome with a heady rush of excitement. There was so much energy to work with. She could do far more than she'd ever imagined. She wove and drew and wove and drew. Kix, catching her excitement, grew interested. He peeped out of her collar to watch her progress.

She could feel the pulsing, vibrant spell she was creating. It dwelled in the broken place in the tree, joining what had been parted, repairing what had been broken. When the weave was complete, she paused to check her work for errors. Then, she released.

The spell flowed out of her, taking energy from Kix and pouring it into the tree. She opened her eyes in time to see a luminous series of lines fill in and become solid.

The wound in the trunk healed. It shut in the space of a few heartbeats, sealing over with new wood and new bark as if it had never been. Marim stepped back and was surprised to feel a rush of vertigo. She set her hand back on the bark to steady herself.

It was then she saw Braven. He stood only a few steps away, watching her with an intense, focused expression. She blinked and looked around.

They were all watching her – at least a dozen Brinlocks who stood in an uneasy cluster amid the torn bodies of the men who'd fallen.

Coll was nowhere to be seen.

✝

Adni trailed Cockram as he crashed around in the woods. Her brother was heading in the wrong direction, blundering along at a frantic jog that wasn't taking him any closer to the edge of the forest. It wasn't difficult to keep pace with him. He was noisy and clumsy, and she could feel the magic of the wood whispering to him, leading him in circles.

As they moved, the night went silent. There were no more screams, no more bellows and crashes. The woods were dark and silver and cool. Cockram ran. Adni followed.

At last, her brother seemed to realize he was lost. Although he and his group of men had walked only a short distance before selecting their trees and raising their axes, he'd been running for many minutes without finding the forest's edge.

He stopped. Adni did as well, watching him from behind a large fern. She could see the white of his wild eye, hear the hoarse panting of his breath. She could hear him whispering as well – a steady stream of words pouring out in a child's prayer, asking for Delari to shine a light on his soul. Whatever that meant.

Adni suspected that even if the goddess could be convinced to do such a thing, she would not like what she saw in Cockram. In the nine months her brother had been incarcerated, Adni had found herself oddly conflicted about what she hoped would happen to him. Up until the night of the mob, she'd always thought she wanted to see her brother suffer and die for his attempt to kill her. That night, she'd done her best to encourage the crowd to turn violent. Seeing Cockram fall as a result of the very anger and hatred he'd sewed had seemed poetic.

Unfortunately, it hadn't quite worked. The City Guard had at last organized itself, arriving on the scene and restoring order before the events of that evening became lethal. She'd watched Cockram as he was clapped in irons and led away.

After that, she'd mostly been curious. Would he emerge from his time in custody a broken man? Would he creep back to the Rooster's Comb and try to pick up life where he'd left off? Or would he emerge angrier than ever, still committed to the fight?

She'd expected the latter, but even she'd been surprised at how quickly he was able to launch this offensive on the forest.

Tonight, Adni had been in Lan Dinas trying to gather intelligence on whether or not the cloister would soon receive a new rector, when she'd caught Braven's thrumming cry for help. She'd hurried for the forest and arrived in time to see Cockram blast free of some entangling magic, and run away. On impulse, she'd followed.

Now, Adni's brother leaned his back against a tree and slid slowly to the ground. His breath was coming in gasps that sounded halfway to sobs. As she watched, he removed his eye patch, wiped at his face, and replaced it again.

Adni fingered the blowgun that hung inside her cloak. She was a good shot, and her poison darts were deadly. She could end it for him before he even knew she was there. She could see the conclusion of his miserable, destructive life.

But she found she didn't want him to die that way. Adni didn't want this terrible man merely killed. She wanted him destroyed. She wanted Cockram brought as low as she'd been the day she learned her own brother had slipped poison into her tea for weeks. The person she'd thought was her best friend had watched her sicken and wither without remorse, his own actions making her grow weak and thin until, finally, she couldn't even get out of bed.

In the forest, an owl hooted. Cockram looked up with a jerk, as if the sound signaled his doom. As if mobilized by the sound, Adni stepped out from behind the fern, throwing back her hood and pushing her cloak behind her shoulders.

Cockram saw her at once. His body went stiff. For a moment, she thought he would spring to his feet. Instead, he folded his arms across his chest. His eyes swept past Adni to rake the woods beyond. He spoke in a strange, wheezy sing-song. "Your trick won't work on me this time, little Tessilari girl. I know my sister is dead. Why not come out where I can see you?"

For one, suspended instant, Adni thought he'd gone mad. The carnage in the woods had unhinged his mind, and now he was raving. She stood a moment, still and silent.

Then, she understood. Cockram wasn't mad. He was simply refusing to believe the evidence of his own eyes. He thought she was an illusion, not his actual sister grown to adulthood despite his attempt on her life.

For some reason, this comprehension filled Adni with anger. She stepped forward, crossing the space between the two of them in a few long strides. He didn't react as she approached, only watched her with a strange, smug stillness. She stooped, raised an arm, and slapped him across his missing eye.

The slap was hard and satisfying. Cockram cursed and stumbled to his feet, reeling back and away from her, his remaining eye wild. She stalked after him, moving with quiet, deliberate fluidity. "I am not an illusion." She was surprised at the venom in her own voice. "I am your sister, you piece of scum. The one you tried to murder."

Cockram was holding a hand over his eyepatch, still trying to retreat. "No." He shook his head. His neck cloth was in disarray, the little pin of the rooster he wore there askew. "It's not possible. It doesn't make sense. If you are Adni and you've been secretly alive all this time, why show up now? Why wait all these years? No. The coincidence it too great. You are the Tessilari girl. You must be. You're wearing a disguise. You're in my head. You're trying to make me think I'm insane." The words tumbled out in a monologue, quick and jumbled, more like he was speaking to himself than to her.

Of all the outcomes Adni could have foreseen, she'd never imagined this one.

Her brother refused to believe she was real.

In his stumbling retreat, Cockram bumped into a tree. Adni stopped as well, trying to decide what to do next. She could kill him anyway, she supposed, but she didn't want him to die not believing in her. She wanted him to know she'd caught up to deliver justice at last.

There was a rustle in the darkness, the whir of small wings on the air. Then, without warning, a tall, slender young man stepped into view. He carried a staff and wore a cloak. A tessila flitted about his head, and there was murder in his eyes.

Adni turned, took one look at the boy's face, and made a snap decision. Before either the Tessilari or Cockram could do anything more, Adni stepped forward and threw her arm around brother's shoulders, so her cloak covered him as well as her. She pulled up her hood and wove an additional passive echo spell to wrap around them. "Stop," she hissed as Cockram tried to pull away from her. "Quiet. Move with me if you want to live."

CHAPTER 4

On fine days, the large, ornate doors of the Hall of the Wheel stood open, a Guardian posted on either side of the entrance. Braven knew both the women who were on duty today, but he did not stop to say hello as he made his exit. He ducked his head as he hurried for the steps leading down to the street. He kept his face oriented ahead, his eyes down.

He'd just been released from the special session of the Wheel that had been called to assess the events of the previous night. He'd been kept for hours, alternately standing and sitting, speaking and waiting. Sometimes he was allowed to overhear the evolving discussion between the screened figures he could not see and whose voices he could not recognize. Sometimes a bubble of magic separated him from the proceedings, and he was left to do nothing but sit and wait.

There had been many questions to answer. Braven had done his best to be factual, concise, and clear. But what had happened in the forest was so nightmarish, so incomprehensible, he'd had trouble, at times, not letting his emotions show. When asked if he'd had any part in the killings, Braven had spoken quickly and firmly. No, he had only summoned illusory dires, hoping to scare the men with axes away. Coll of the Tessilari had done all the killing. Well, not Coll, precisely. His tessila, Wip.

Even as he spoke these words, however, Braven felt oddly uneasy. It was true, he hadn't killed anyone last night. But he had killed. He'd never reported that first incident in the forest, the man whose axe he'd caused to slip. Adni hadn't either. She'd been as good as her word, as far as that went. He hadn't been keeping it a secret, exactly. He just hadn't told anyone what had happened.

Now, he felt he could not. It also felt strangely cowardly to point the finger at Coll. True, the carnage in the woods had been shocking and terrible, but as he hurried down the street, making for the edge of town, Braven had to admit he felt those men had earned their deaths.

The street grew crowded. Braven threw up the hint of a passive echo spell – not enough to really conceal him, just enough to encourage anyone who might be inclined to speak with him to move on by. Braven had answered enough questions for one day.

He hadn't been entirely conscious of where he was going until he found his feet on the trail that led out the north end of Gol Ledrith. He was traveling fast. It felt good to walk, to do something as simple and uncomplicated as put one foot in front of another. Soon he was climbing up the slight slope of the mountain. A while later, he reached the stone circle and its four pillars. There, he paused.

The door in the mountainside stood open. Two Guardians were now posted here as well. Braven dropped his passive echo spell. It was illegal to use magic to pass a guard.

Krail was the more senior of those posted here, one of the most respected of the Guardians. He gave Braven a short nod. "Where you headed, lad?"

"I wanted to visit Carreg Dinas. May I use the passage?"

Krail's eyes were gray and somber. Braven had no doubt the older man knew what had happened in the woods last night, and had heard rumors of Braven's part in those events. There was a beat of silence before he answered. "The Fog Dial and the Library are off limits to all citizens until the Wheel determines their significance, but you may pass through to the other side of the mountain."

The swell of gratitude and relief Braven felt when he heard the words was excessive. It struck him he was exhausted, his emotions strained and ready to snap. He'd barely slept the previous night, even after he'd been cleared to return to his home. He'd been called before the Wheel at dawn. Now, it was early afternoon.

The tunnel was dim and full of echoes. Braven walked quickly, giving the Guardians posted by the doors to the library and fog room the briefest of nods as he strode past. He was through the mountain and out the other side in less time than seemed possible.

It was a fine day in Carreg Dinas. The abandoned city lay within its sheer wrapping of fog, the white stone of the houses luminous and brilliant under the muffled sun. Out in the harbor, the Tessilari ship waited like a ghost. Sails down, it sat at anchor. Its presence made a curl of unease drift through Braven, indistinct but unsettling. Were there more Tessilari aboard? Were they all capable of the kind of destruction Braven had witnessed last night? How many Tessilari would it take to depopulate this island and claim it for their own?

Braven turned and walked towards the square that stood at the center of the city, with its benches and ornate, empty fountain. He wished there was water in these canals, that Gia could follow him here when he came, swimming along beside him and cheeping at him every now and then. She was back in Gol Ledrith at the moment, sleeping in a stand of reeds.

Braven should be sleeping too. Instead, he continued, his steps slowing as he neared the central square. As he rounded the last bend in the road and looked ahead, he was surprised to see it wasn't empty. A figure sat on one of the benches, slim, with shorn hair.

It was Marim. Braven felt a strange lurch in his chest when he saw her. He remembered her as she'd been in the woods the night before, moving from tree to tree, pouring healing power into each damaged trunk. By the time she'd finished, it was as if the men and their axes had never been. Except for the bodies, anyway. So many bodies, strewn and sprawling, some already crawling with busy ants.

Coll had killed the men from Lan Dinas. Marim had healed the trees. Now, looking at her, Braven could see she was tired. He knew she'd been called before the Wheel that morning as well. Sealed off in her own chamber, she'd most likely been speaking when he'd been told to wait. Coll had been summoned too, but Braven knew nothing of what the Wheel had asked the others.

Braven moved across the square and settled himself on the bench next to Marim. She looked up at him. She wore a blouse with a high collar, as she always did, but it was unbuttoned and smoothed down, her throat bare in the weak light. The scarring around her neck was a silver web over her otherwise smooth, pale skin. He wondered at the marks. What had happened to her to mark her so? If she could heal so many trees of such significant damage, surely she should have been able to heal her own wounds before they hardened into scars.

Marim's eyes were rimmed in red. She wiped at them as he arranged his cloak on the bench. Kix, clinging to Marim's sleeve and looking strangely deflated, only gave Braven one half-hearted hiss.

They said nothing for a time. Braven could hear the distant sigh and crash of the ocean and smell the brine on the air. A stilt-legged bird landed on the lip of the fountain, cocked its head at them, and flew away.

Marim sighed—a shaky sound—and raised her eyes to look at Braven. "I've known him since he was a boy. A little boy, alone and terrified."

Braven raised his eyes. He could see the bulky shape of the ship in the harbor. He understood, then, that something irrevocable had happened last night. A stone had been dropped down the side of the mountain. It would loose another stone, and they'd tumble together, knocking sand and gravel free, cascading down and down in an avalanche of change.

He didn't know what to say, didn't know what any of it meant, or what the landscape would look like when the slide was finished. He squinted into the muffled sun. "The men who died in those woods were children once as well." It was all he could think to say.

The stone bench was hard and cold. Marim felt she'd been sitting here for a long time. She wasn't sure why she'd come to Carreg Dinas when she'd been released from the Hall of the Wheel. She wasn't sure why it felt good to sit in the abandoned square and try not to remember the cries and the screams and the way Coll had stood there and held his staff on the ground and watched with avid eyes as Wip ripped every man holding an axe to pieces.

One had gotten away. Marim had thought Coll hadn't noticed. She'd seen the shadow jogging through the trunks, and tried to distract him with telling him to stop. She'd thought it had worked. Until she'd looked up after healing the first tree to find him gone.

They'd called for him, but to no avail. Eventually they found him back in Gol Ledrith, sleeping in his borrowed house as if nothing at all had happened.

Now, sitting with Braven, Marim felt undone. She felt as if she'd failed, somehow. For much of Coll's childhood, he'd come to her with his questions and his troubles. She'd been the one to explain to him about right and wrong, to try to show him love and compassion.

And now, he'd done this.

She looked at Braven. Dark moons discolored the skin beneath his eyes. His cloak was stained and rumpled. "What would you have done? What would your people have done, if Coll hadn't stepped in?"

She thought it a significant question. She'd learned during her hearing that nineteen bodies had been discovered in the woods. Each man had come into the woods bearing an axe and a torch, prepared to work together to bring down as many of the great trees as they could, as quickly as possible. Had Marim been alone, she'd not have been able to stop them. She didn't know if Braven could have, either. Someone, the ringleader, had known the dires were only illusions.

If the men had managed to fell a tree before reinforcements arrived, what then? It would have changed how the people of Lan Dinas viewed the forest. Forever.

Braven rubbed a hand through his pale hair, leaving it sticking up in all directions to catch the strange light. His face had a light tan – or at least what passed for one here in this place where fog always shrouded the land. She'd never noticed the light dusting of freckles across the bridge of his nose before. She felt a sudden, unexpected swell of gratitude towards Braven. He'd been a good friend to her. First, that night in Embriem's house, he hadn't tried to leave her behind even though he'd most likely suffered consequences for bringing in the first outsider to see Gol Ledrith in centuries. When it emerged how badly her magic had muddled Embriem, he'd stood up for her, explaining how dire a situation they'd been in, defending her with his opinion she'd made an honest mistake.

Now, even after standing in the dark woods and watching a Tessila mow through men like a fox slaughters hens in a coop, he sat with her in the quiet of the empty city, talking to her as if nothing between them had changed.

But things had changed. Treyam and Jey had come to sue for peace, but why was Coll here? He'd come because of Marim. He was not an official representative of the Tessilari, but that wouldn't make much difference to those his actions had affected.

Braven drew in a long breath through his nostrils, rubbing at a small cut on his thumb. "I don't know, honestly. They weren't afraid of my dires, not really. I might have been able to …" he cut off, shaking his head. "This has never happened before."

Out in the harbor, seagulls wheeled and cried. Marim felt a strange heat building behind her eyes. She spoke with the quiet conviction she'd carried in her heart since her childhood, since the day she'd woken up to learn there was a war to fight, and she'd caused it. "It's me," she said. "Wherever I go, I bring trouble. Not just trouble. Disaster. Everything I do when I'm trying to do good, it ends up twisted and dark and terrible. Even Coll, now. All these years, I thought I was something he needed, a good influence. I thought I could help guide him into a happy life, in spite of what happened when he was a child. But he came here because of me. He killed all those men because of me."

She stopped, aware how hysterical she must sound. She expected Braven to refute her, to argue with her the way Liam did when she tried to express this feeling.

Next to her, Braven shifted. He smelled like the woods, like crushed leaves and loam and dew. She didn't turn to look at him, too afraid of what she'd see in his eyes, so it startled her when she felt his fingers brush, light and tentative, against her scarred neck.

Marim felt a strange frisson of energy. She froze, going rigid, even forgetting to breath.

Inexplicably, Kix did not react at all.

Braven's hand fell away after only the briefest touch. His voice was low and tired. "Sometimes you do something because it's the only thing you can do, in the moment. Sometimes what feels like the right thing turns out to be the wrong one. We can't know, ever, where our choices will lead us. We can only take our best guess, and hope."

Marim wondered what moments were in his mind, what choices he wished he could go back and undo. She tried to think of something more to say, but her mind was blank, wiped clean by his touch.

Braven continued. "If you hadn't released the Diod, the Tessilari would not have saved Masidon. They wouldn't have had any bargaining chips with which to forge an alliance. They would still be hidden, hunted, reviled. Like we are."

A breeze swept in from the sea, swirling the fog and blowing Marim's hair into her face. She pushed it back, surprised Braven had such a complete understanding of the War of Diodsfall – its causes and outcomes, and even her roll in it.

Braven shrugged. "You didn't start a war, Marim. You didn't kill those men last night. You're just a tiny piece in all of this, like the rest of us."

The breeze stirred again, stronger this time. Marim looked up to see a bank of clouds to the south, dark and towering and somehow ominous. She remembered the storms from the year before, the way they seemed to be attracted to the island when the seasons came. She tried to remember how those had looked when they'd rolled in.

Braven, following her gaze, looked up as well. "Do storms often come from the south?" Marim asked.

His brow furrowing, Braven stood. The wind caught the tail of his cloak and whipped it around his legs. "No," he said. "Never."

Aldrath opened the door into the quiet apartment, gesturing for his guest to go ahead. Treyam of the Tessilari walked around him, the hem of his long coat shifting and swaying about his legs. Aldrath shut the door and turned in time to see Embriem sink back into his chair, the spark of hope dying in his face.

He knew he would receive no response, but he spoke anyway. "Embriem, I've brought someone to see you. Someone who might be able to help."

Before the arrival of the Tessilari, Aldrath had been on the point of trying one of several risky experiments to see if he couldn't wrestle the active persuasion spell free of Embriem's psyche. But some intuition had counseled him to wait. At one of the many social events put on by the Brinlocks in honor of the Tessilari, he'd ended up in a conversation with Treyam, discussing the distinctions between passive and active magics.

It was no surprise, of course, that the teachings of the Tessilari and the Brinlocks differed considerably, both in terms of theory and practice. Some of this was purely philosophical – a different way of looking at the same thing. Increasingly, however, as he studied Marim's magic, Aldrath was forming the opinion that the very energy she used in her spellwork was different from his own.

His few conversations with Marim, however, had revealed she was no scholar. She'd grown embarrassed and flustered when he tried to speak with her about more abstract concepts, so he'd given up trying.

Treyam, however, was a different story. It had taken only minutes for he and Aldrath to segue past pleasantries and onto meatier topics, such as Embriem's predicament.

The Tessilari had shown immediate and keen interest. "Active persuasion," Treyam had said. "I suppose I can grasp the theory, but I've never heard of it being done. It would require some kind of connection – a way to bypass the natural defenses of the psyche."

Aldrath, surprised, went on to explain it was a Tessilari who had cast the spell, and now could not seem to undo its effects. Treyam had grown even more interested. Ignoring the groups of nearby people hoping for a chance to make his acquaintance, he sipped from his short glass of tiin. "The spell hasn't worn off on its own? What's sustaining it? An active casting would take a good deal of energy to linger so long."

Nearby, a group of young ladies jostled and giggled as they eyed Coll, who stood alone before a window, looking out. "Embriem sustains the spell with his own magic. It's hooked into him. His desire to fuel the spell is as strong as his obsession with the caster, and the effort is sapping his brinlin. I don't think she'll survive much longer if we cannot intervene."

Treyam looked fascinated. He swirled his drink in its glass. "You say Marim did this? Our Marim?" As he spoke he glanced about the room, as if looking for the young woman. Aldrath saw her approaching Coll, carrying two drinks.

Before Aldrath could answer, Treyam tossed back the rest of his tiin, looked at Aldrath and said, "Look. I don't want to be presumptuous. I'm sure you've got as good a grasp on the situation as anyone. But might I have a look at this man?"

And so, here they were. The visit had been delayed by the events that had unfolded in the forest only a short time after that conversation. Aldrath had been required to sit in his place on the Wheel and try, with the others, to come to a decision about what should be done.

Coll had been released, but he'd been assigned a shadow squad of six Guardians – their best in the arts of moving unseen. They would take rotating shifts so two would stay near him at all times, reporting and recording his movements.

Meanwhile, the Wheel was ferociously divided, and had adjourned without reaching any decision about what to do. Aldrath himself was of the mind that Braven had called for help, and Coll had answered that call. Yes, his response had been excessive, but he'd grown up in the recent aftermath of a war where acts of terrible violence against people who could wield magics were illegal, but not uncommon. In their questioning of

Marim, they'd learned of the terrible trauma he'd suffered in his own childhood.

When called upon to explain himself, Coll had stood before the Wheel, composed but subdued, and said he'd been told the trees were sacred. He'd understood this to mean they must be defended at all costs. He had only done what seemed necessary, and was sorry if he'd misunderstood.

Aldrath thought the young man's words were genuine. Others on the Wheel did not agree. Some felt there was no justification for the deaths of nineteen men who had not, in fact, shown any inclination to harm other humans. Cutting down trees, in the view of those who had been doing it, was not a crime of any kind. There was no formal treaty between the people of Lan Dinas and the Brinlocks, because the people of Lan Dinas did not know the Brinlocks existed. The forest was avoided because it scared them, not because they understood its significance.

These were valid points, and Aldrath was at odds even within himself. More importantly, no one could guess what might happen next – how the people of Lan Dinas might respond to such losses.

For now, Aldrath could only put it out of his mind. He would meditate on that problem later. For now, he had another to face.

Treyam, moving towards the chair where Embriem sat, looked down at its occupant with keen eyes. Aldrath approached as well, feeling his heart settle a little heavier at the sight of Embriem. The man had been thin when he'd arrived here, but now he was deflated. It was as if, day by day, he lost another sliver of his animating force. His vitality was draining away, along with his will to live.

"Embriem, this is Treyam. He's from Masidon. From Deramor itself. He's a representative of the Tessilari, come to sue for peace." It was odd, how one could not seem to dispense with social conventions, even when they were so patently useless. Embriem did not respond to Aldrath's words in any way. His eyes stayed fixed on the view out the window – the bridges, rooftops, and streets of Gol Ledrith.

Treyam stepped forward. "Nice to meet you, Embriem."

Still no response. Aldrath pulled up a chair for Treyam, and the two of them sat down together, considering the wasted man with his sunken eyes. "May I?" Treyam extended a hand towards Embriem's arm, and Aldrath nodded.

As Treyam set his hand on Embriem's, a feeble hiss sounded behind them, coming from the stand of reeds that grew from the elevated pool in the corner. Aldrath felt his heart turn over with sorrow. The man's brinlin was nearly as weak and wasted as he was, but still, she tried to defend him. He spoke a few soothing words to her, but did not approach the pool. Doing so would only stress the animal further.

He waited, listening to the steady sound of Embriem's breathing. Treyam's tessila, brilliant white in color with gold tips, peeped her sharp head out from the man's collar. If the stories the Brinlock Watchers collected in town could be believed, this man was a Peace Warden: a designation of Tessilari Aldrath did not fully understand. All he knew was this man's unique power had enabled an aged Tessilari to draw near to the Diod. Then, she'd sacrificed her life to destroy the creature, and save Masidon.

Treyam did not particularly look like a hero as he sat with his hand on Embriem's. Aldrath, not wanting to stare, returned his gaze to the window. He'd just noticed the fog that clung to the trees on the mountainside was unusually restless when Treyam said, "There are two spells here, woven together. One in hers – tessila magic for certain. The other is his, I think. The magic has a tenor I cannot quite grasp onto. They are knit together, passing energy back and forth. I think if I focus on one and you the other, perhaps we could unravel them at the same time, and set him free."

The morning a wood cutter discovered nineteen corpses laid out at the edge of the forest, Cockram woke up in his bed. He lay for a moment, disoriented as the weak dawn light sifted in through the windows. His blinds had not been drawn.

That was strange. Cockram shifted in his sheets and caught a whiff of smoke. Not the wholesome smoke of reed fire, but the tarry, inky smell of torches.

It all came back in a rush. The woods, the smack smack of axes chopping into bark. All those months in prison, he'd worked on his plan, refining it, honing it, gathering participants. He'd thought if they could bring one tree down, just one, the mystique of the woods would be broken. The people of Lan Dinas would see how childish their superstitions were.

Why he hated the woods with such venom was a question Cockram refused to consider closely. He hated the woods the same way he hated the lake and the tiny monsters that lived in the reeds. He hated them because they called to him, had always called to him. His sister had succumbed to that call, but he was stronger than she was. He'd resisted all these years.

The thought of Adni made Cockram sit bolt upright in bed. He'd convinced himself the first time he saw her, on the docks the night he'd raised his mob, that she'd been a trick – something the Tessilari girl cooked up to unnerve him.

But last night.

Memories flooded him. The magic gripping his legs. The screaming. The bellows of some huge monster, the guttering light of the torches. The torn bodies, everywhere.

He'd managed to escape, to tear himself free of the magic that held all the other men still. He'd run, but he'd been pursued.

Adni. Adni had caught up to him. They'd spoken, argued. Another man had appeared. She'd thrown her cloak around him and then …

He couldn't remember. He couldn't remember the walk back to town, didn't recall returning to the Rooster's Comb, undressing, getting in bed.

But he knew one thing. Adni was his sister. He felt the certainty of that knowledge running deep. It was rooted in his soul as surely as his own sense of self. When he'd felt her arm around his shoulder, heard her familiar voice in his ear, he knew there was no magic on earth that could be so convincing.

He also knew something else. It was less about knowledge and more to do with understanding. Cockram understood, suddenly, that Adni was not dead. She was not dead because someone had helped her escape from the room where she should have been given the death serum – just as someone had helped Marim and Embriem and Tassin disappear from the house when the mob had gathered around. The help could not have come from Lan Dinas. Cockram was too aware of the rhythms of the city, its underbelly, the face it presented to the world. There was no secret society of magical practitioners hiding within its streets.

Twice now, men who had gone into the forest to chop down trees had been killed. They hadn't been attacked by wild animals. They hadn't gotten lost. One had impossibly chopped his own leg instead of a tree. The others had been torn apart by a massive, enraged monster.

There was only one explanation. The woods were not empty, as everyone in Lan Dinas believed. There were people living there – people who could wield magics, people who had spirited his sister away the night she should have died, people who had allowed his Adni to turn into an abomination.

This understanding formed in Cockram, hot and quick, almost as soon as he woke. It filled him with energy. He heaved himself out of bed. He wasn't properly undressed. He still wore his trousers and his shirt. His boots, vest, belt, and scarf lay in a heap on the floor. It was unnerving not to be able to remember what had happened last night.

He stripped, then dressed again in fresh clothing. His golden rooster pin had fallen to the floor. He almost missed it in the shadows under the bed. Only because he stepped on it as he reached for his boots did he find it again. He picked it up, poked it into his neck scarf, and felt his sense of certainty grow.

There were people in the woods, and they were evil. So far, Cockram had only tried to fight them with axes and men. He needed a better weapon, he saw now. He needed a method of offense teeth could not bite, and claws could not rend.

The answer, he saw, was fire. He could start a fire in the reeds and guide it towards the forest. Trees and ferns would burn, and the people of Lan Dinas would see what the flames flushed out of the forest.

CHAPTER 5

Vailria couldn't remember how long it had been since she'd first noticed the sparks. The days had a way of blurring together, twilight shifting into dawn, one moon phase becoming another.

She'd noticed it, she thought, around the time she'd first seen the Tessilari ship. It was that vessel that had made her stand on her outcropping for longer than usual, squinting into the glare of sunlight on water, trying to figure out if there was any chance the ship might come her way.

From her position on her little island, Vailria had been able to see the five great pillars that blocked access to the abandoned harbor of Carreg Dinas. She recalled the morning she saw, with shock, that the massive stones had disappeared. It astonished her to think the Brinlocks had found a way to open their sheltered cove, even more bizarre to realize they'd done so to let the Tessilari in.

Had that been before or after the first time she paused, squinted, and took in the strange flickering light in the sky at the summit of the craggy mountain? That first time, she'd stood for a long while, watching the strange shifting, flaring glow. The light was fitful, like a glowfly at the end of its life. And the fog. The fog was attracted to it in strange ways. It swirled around the peak now, teasing itself into flowing shapes as if trying to woo the light in an effort at courtship.

Now, every time Vailria looked out over the ocean, she couldn't help but let her eyes stray towards the rocky peak of Cynnes Tarth. This morning was no different. As Vailria walked, barefoot, across the sun-warmed rock and turned to gaze out to sea more out of habit than hope, she saw two things that made her heart stutter.

First, a vessel. Initially, she thought it far in the distance, for it was small against the rearing, fog shrouded cliffs of the backside of Cynnes Tarth. She squinted, her eyes adjusting, and realized it was closer than she'd believed. This was no multi-masted trade vessel, but a small, agile sailboat, cutting through the glassy ocean, heading straight for her beach.

Although she was alone except for a few pecking seabirds, she spoke his name aloud. "Tommin." It had to be. At last, he was coming to make good on his promise. At last, they would begin to build their life here, tucked away on this little spit of land nobody cared about but them.

Vailria was so overcome with a rush of emotion, she almost didn't notice the second thing. In the glare of the early sun, the light on that distant summit would have been easy to overlook.

But as Vailria shaded her eyes to gaze hungrily across the waves, trying to make out the figure of a man on the light ship's deck, the clouds drew her attention. They were wispy things, drawn on a high, thin breeze. But they seemed to be massing around the top of the island where they caught and amplified that strange, leaping light.

Even then, Vailria might have missed the signs. She was so overwhelmed with happiness to see Tommin, so thrilled at the speed with which his light vessel cut through the smooth sea, she had all but forgotten anything but her relief by the time the light sailboat dropped anchor and Tommin, laughing, paddled himself ashore on a flatboard.

Vailria's life had not contained many moments of pure happiness. Of the ones she could recall, most of them revolved around this man. Their first kiss, shy and quick. The first night she'd stayed aboard his vessel with him, when he'd asked her to marry him and she'd refused on the grounds that they could not be together. They'd been young then, barely adults, full of giddy, uncomplicated love.

None of those previous moments could hold a candle to this one.

Tommin was weathered now, his skin made rough by salt and wind, his eyes full of the things he'd seen on his hard crossings. Still, he laughed like a boy as he splashed through the breakers, flung his oar aside, and caught her in his arms.

For a few minutes, anyway, there was no room in Vailria's mind for anything but joy. His beard scratched her neck. She breathed in the scent of him – salt and sun and wind. She laughed and cried as he kissed her mouth, wrapping his ropy arms around her waist to carry her up the sandy beach.

He drew back, smiling down. "Sorry I was so long coming. I found the vessel quick enough, but she needed repairs. It was murder, getting the timber. Everyone told me I was crazy when I set out this morning, what with the unnatural storm brewing. But the sea's calm enough for now, and I couldn't leave you here to face that monster alone."

As he spoke, Tommin nodded his chin to the far southern horizon.

Vailria turned, and her heart gave a little lurch.

There was a build of towering purple clouds on the sky, creeping towards Cynnes Tarth from the south. It was a massive construction of a storm, lightning dancing in its depths. And the trail of wispy clouds she'd noticed led from the building thunderhead straight to the summit of Cynnes Tarth.

Tommin was still talking, explaining he needed to make the ship fast and find the best place for her to ride out the storm.

But Vailria wasn't listening. She was shaking her head, staring at the horizon. "No," she said, certainty building in her by the instant. "We can't stay here, Tommin. That storm isn't natural. It isn't right. Cynnes Tarth has called it into existence." She turned, pointing at the collected darkness around the light on the peaks.

Tommin frowned, looking in the direction she indicated. She continued, her own sense of certainty growing as she spoke. "It's not going to pass over us like a normal storm. Once it reaches us, it will linger. Something has happened. I have been seeing sparks in the sky for weeks now. Perhaps the Brinlocks have woken some magic in the mountain. But the island's magic is broken, as everyone knows. If no one's been up to the summit, they might not realize what's happening. We have to go back. We have to go now. We have to beat that storm to Cynnes Tarth."

"Collaborative casting." Treyam spoke in a speculative tone, turning the glass of chilled tiin slowly in his hands. The day was warm for the season, the air heavy. The fog was thick and restless, smelling of damp foliage and the weedy shallows of the warmlake beneath the peculiar rusty tang it always carried.

Aldrath and Treyam sat on Aldrath's private balcony, which was high and broad, built out over the water. Both men were tired, but after their success with Embriem, they felt a strange reluctance to part.

Aldrath felt the pleasant blend of fatigue and satisfaction that always came over him in the aftermath of working particularly difficult magics. Even with Treyam's help, the work with Embriem hadn't been easy. But when he'd narrowed his focus down to only the brinlin fueled side of the spell, Aldrath had found a place to begin. As Treyam had done the same on the other strand, Aldrath's path had only become more clear. As they'd worked, their weavings of dissolution had blended somehow, uniting into a single, harmonious work made to unravel the active persuasion spell.

When they'd at last released their weaving, they'd done so with confidence. Their spell had taken hold of Marim's working and unspun its threads as neatly as a dropped spool uncoils its thread. It had taken but a moment before all the magic was gone, blended back into the air as if it had never been.

Embriem had drawn in a sharp breath and sat up, blinking. With wild eyes, he'd stared at his two companions, both slightly woozy in the aftermath of their effort. He'd narrowed his eyes, his gaze bouncing from one to the other. He'd spoken in a tone Aldrath had never heard him use before. Direct, focused, and forceful. "Who are you? Why am I here? Where is Tassin, my son? And Nel."

In the reeds, the man's brinlin had given a cheep of pure joy and thrown herself into the water to swim with as much energy as her feeble body could muster to the point in the basin closest to Embriem. She'd begun to bob alarmingly, having trouble fighting the mild current, but Embriem had rushed out of his chair and gone to her, scooping her out of the water. Tears in his eyes, voice choked, he'd stared down at her wasted body in total confusion. "My Nel. What's happened to you?"

Aldrath had gone to the door, then, and sent a message for the healer. He explained everything as best he could, watching the play of emotions across Embriem's face as he tried to account for months of lost time.

At last, the healer arrived and took over, shooing Aldrath and Treyam out the door.

The Brinlock and the Tessilari hadn't spoken as they'd left Embriem's apartment, but it had seemed unthinkable they would part before they'd had a chance to discuss what had just happened. Aldrath led the way to his own home, asked his people to prepare cold tiin, and they'd retired to the balcony to sit in a silence that felt entirely natural until the drinks were brought up and they were left alone again.

Now, Treyam continued. "It's not a new idea. We do it all the time in Masidon. Almost every working of any significance requires more than one mage. But this was different. This was … bigger." He trailed off, as if wishing for words their language did not possess. His accent struck Aldrath as sharp, somehow, but not in an unpleasant way. According to hearsay, Treyam had grown up in the Valley of Mist – the Tessilari retreat that had been more well-hidden and isolated from Deramor than even Gol Ledrith was from Lan Dinas.

Aldrath thought he knew what the man was getting at. When they'd worked together, it was as if the strands of magic they wove and fitted into place complimented one another, like the tenor softening and strengthening the soprano.

On the edge of the patio stood a pool with reeds. Hob popped out of the water doing a backflip, showing off. Aldrath smiled gently in his direction. "A choir does not sing with one voice," he suggested. "Music is strengthened by harmonies."

Sitting forward, Treyam nodded. Judging from his face, Aldrath would have placed the man in his late thirties. His hair was short and smooth, with a few scattered gray hairs around the temples. But he knew better than to judge the age of a Tessilari by looking. "Yes, exactly. It makes me wonder what could be accomplished if our peoples worked together."

Abruptly, Aldrath thought of the men who had died only the previous night, killed by a tessila. He'd gone into the forest to see the carnage with his own eyes, arriving with a late party after cleanup was already underway. The Brinlocks had done what they could to tidy and clean the dead, carried them out of the woods, and left them for the people of Lan Dinas to find. Some of the men had died of unseen injuries – snapped necks, crushed spines. Others had been torn apart by talons and teeth. Some were missing limbs. One corpse had lacked a head. Based on the size and extent of the wounds, the tessila that had done the damage must have been huge.

Collaboration was all well and good until it met with difference of opinion or misaligned viewpoints. Out of the corner of his eye, Aldrath saw Hob scuttle up a reed. His smooth, damp body was so soft, so vulnerable in comparison to the scaled hide of a tessila.

Following Aldrath's gaze, Treyam turned and regarded the brinlin for a time, a smile twitching up the corner of his mouth. "Can they shift?" he said. "Change size, I mean, like our tessili can?"

Aldrath looked for the man's tessila, but it was nowhere in evidence. He did notice the presence of a thin metal ring hanging on the outside of the man's shirt. He'd seen Marim wearing something similar, and felt the magic in the artifact.

Aldrath hesitated. On the one hand, his recent experience with Treyam made him feel a closeness to the man. He was inclined to answer the question honestly, to hold nothing back.

On the other hand, there was reality to contend with. If Aldrath revealed their weaknesses, the Tessilari would know how great a power advantage he and his people really had.

Aldrath leaned back in his chair, sipping his tiin. "Have you not heard the tales of sea monsters large enough to drag even the most massive of trade ships to the bottom of the ocean? Where do you think such stories come from?"

It wasn't a lie. Old records indicated brinlins had once possessed the same power as the tessili. The most powerful among them had been able to expand into beasts larger than even the massive whales that migrated past the islands every spring. But that power had been lost with the cracking of Cynnes Tarth, and the resultant division of the warmlake.

Treyam didn't answer. Aldrath turned in time to see a flicker of something in his eyes. Regret? Disappointment?

The heavy air swirled, bringing with it a creeping tendril of unexpected cold. It traced up Aldrath's neck, making him shiver. At the same moment, he heard a pounding below, and a shout. "We need to speak with Aldrath. Please. Is anyone here?"

That was when he raised his eyes and saw the storm.

The fog was ragged. It snagged and swirled as Marim and Braven stood on the outcropping of rock and stared out over the water. In the distance, they could make out the small humped outlines of the other islands. Marim knew from studying the map aboard the vessel that had brought her across from Masidon that there were dozens upon dozens of them in this string, but only a small percentage were large enough to support much of a population.

Marim had thought when she'd set out on this journey that she would see those other islands. Instead, she'd found the secret heart of this one. Now, watching the storm build, she couldn't help but wonder if she'd ever leave this place. There was roiling, dancing magic in the thunderheads – alive and malevolent. "What do you think's causing it?" Marim asked.

Braven, cloak pulled in tight around his body, shook his head. "I have no idea."

Marim, however, thought she knew. Or rather, she thought she understood the sequence of events that had brought the storm into existence. And, as usual when terrible circumstances began to unspool, she was at the heart of the reason why.

"I disrupted something." She felt a strange stillness as she spoke, a sad sense of resignation. This was her curse. "I reawakened the old magic in the mountain. I opened the path to Carreg Dinas. But there's a flaw in that magic, and it's attracting that." She thrust her chin at the roiling thunderhead.

In all her time on this island, Marim had never experienced true cold. Even during the winter, the warmlake never froze. The fog carried a damp flush of warmth. In Masidon, winter was a time of hard ground and snowfall, icy breath and toasty hearths. Not here. Though the trees turned and shed their leaves, though the days grew short and the nights long, the air was never frozen.

Now, she felt the brush of cold air against her cheek. As the fog met the icy air that came with the storm, it shredded into ragged tendrils.

Braven glanced at her, his expression unreadable. Feeling a strange twinge of conviction, she went on. "You didn't believe me earlier, when I said I cause disasters. But it's true. On the way over, sailing from Masidon, the ship's globe began to wobble after the first trial. It was one of the reasons the captain took me on. The magic had become prone to malfunction. He thought I'd be able to help sustain his globe for a few more trips."

Out over the water, the storm was coming, black clouds throwing their shadows across the waves. Braven shifted, tension coming into his body. He was listening, but only half. Part of his attention was elsewhere.

"I touched the globe," Marim said. "Barely touched it. I didn't weave any magic at all, didn't try to change anything. But it gave off this huge spark, and went dead. Completely dead."

Braven did look at her then, eyes wide with surprise. "This was when you were between the Two Trials? How did you make landfall again?"

Marim shivered, remembering the sense of terrible foreboding that had settled over the sailors when they saw what she had done. Some were angry and wanted vengeance, but Captain Tommin wouldn't hear of any kind of retribution. He'd set his mates to guard her door. The crew had stowed the sails and dropped the sea anchor.

For three days, the ship had wallowed and Marim had frantically poured through her spellbook for any kind of weaving that might help. Lookouts were posted around the clock, red lanterns lit on deck. They rationed food and water and begged Delari for a miracle. Their only hope, they'd believed, was to attract the attention of another ship making the crossing.

Marim pushed the memory of those long, long days out of her mind. She went on. "Three days later, the globe came alive again, fully functional. A few days after that, we reached the Island Trial and sliced through without difficulty. But things were never right again with the sailors. They were forever watching me with dark expressions, and making warding gestures at Kix. When we reached Lan Dinas, the captain put me off with half the pay he'd been going to furnish for my services as healer for the entire trip. He was that keen to be rid of me. So I headed for town, and that's where Embriem found me. I tried to save his son's life. You've seen where that ended."

Marim knew she was wallowing in self-pity. She knew she was taking events that weren't about her and making them seem as if they were. Braven seemed to have lost interest in her story again. He was staring out past the harbor mouth with a look of such intensity, Marim turned to look as well.

It took her a moment to see the ship. It was small, with only one, narrow sail, and it was racing before the chill wind like a deer fleeing a fire. As Marim and Braven watched, it shot like an arrow towards the open harbor. Braven said, "It must have come from another island."

Behind them, Marim heard a crackle. She turned to see a shower of red sparks lighting up the sky over Gol Ledrith. As she stared, confused, she heard the note of a deep, throaty gong ringing from far, far in the distance.

Braven's face went a little pale. "It's the muster call. All Keepers and Guardians are being called to battle. But what we're fighting, I have no idea."

He was gone, then, without another word to her, striding away into the ripped fog. She didn't know if he expected her to follow or not, but Marim couldn't help but feel she'd be better off staying out of the way.

So she hung back, watching Braven disappear. Then she turned back to the sea.

The little ship was close now, slewing into the harbor, its sail thrumming before the wind. Marim could make out a man and a woman on the slim deck. With a start of surprise, she recognized them both. It was Vailria and Captain Tommin – the two people who'd stood aboard a ship as it drew away from the docks, leaving her behind to face a mob.

For most of his life, Cockram had avoided the warmlake. When he'd been a child, the other boys had loved to play in the shallows, to chase brinlins and play hide and seek in the fog. Cockram had never joined in those games. Even then, he saw now, he'd had an instinctive understanding of the lake's evil nature.

Only something evil could be so tempting. The lake was always there, a burr at the edge of his consciousness, an itch he could not scratch. Whenever he strayed close to its waters, they seemed to sing to him, inviting him in, holding out some tantalizing, wordless promise.

It was why he'd used his wife's money to build the pub up by the harbor. The salt water did not sing to him. There were no brinlins on the docks. In the years since he'd lost his sister, he'd only gone down to the lakeshore a handful of times.

That was a mistake, he saw now. Avoiding a problem was not the way to solve it. All these years, he'd thought he could dodge his sister's fate if he was only careful. Now that he knew his sister wasn't dead after all, that she'd been lurking nearby, infested with the darkness that tirelessly attempted to reach its tendrils into his own soul, he could not hide any longer.

He was certain that was why Adni hadn't killed him. She'd brought him out of the forest when everyone else had died because she still hoped to turn him. She wanted him to become what she was — a corrupt vessel, filled with unholy power.

It wasn't to be bourn. Cockram had tried to warn the people of Lan Dinas, and they'd thrown him in prison. He'd tried to lead a few brave men to victory, and they'd only died. He saw now with the clarity of hindsight that this was his war. It always had been. He could only win if he fought alone.

The fog was restless as Cockram slipped out the back door of the Rooster's Comb and opened the storage shed in the back yard. Inside, tucked up against one wall, lay a stack of torches: leftovers from his preparations to go into the woods. Cockram bundled as many under his arm as he could carry, pocketed a box of matches, and slammed the shed door closed.

He didn't notice the cold wind as he walked, didn't register the deserted streets. Something had taken hold inside him — a deep sense of certainty.

Cockram walked straight to the warmlake and stopped on the shrouded shore. He stood a moment, breathing in the scent of the shallows, the warm fog, and the pitch in the torches.

He was ready. It was time.

He worked with precision, staking each torch into the reeds, spacing them a few feet apart. As he worked, the brinlins in the reeds cheeped and cried, jumping off their perches to plop into the water. They swarmed along the shore, too many to count. Cockram didn't let himself look at them, though he felt the familiar desire to stop what he was doing and wade into the shallows.

By the time the torches were placed, the air had taken on a strange chill Cockram didn't feel. He was sweating, breathing fast. He reached into his vest and drew out his flint.

The first torch lit with a whoosh. Flames leapt immediately into the reeds. The brinlins were agitated now, calling to one another, scurrying up and down stalks. With a grim smile, Cockram lit the next torch, and the next. Soon they were all burning, the smoke rising to mingle with the fog.

Satisfied, Cockram stepped back. The fires cracked and leapt, throwing heat and light against his face. The cold wind buffeted him, and he felt it at last. He looked up to see the dark clouds in the sky. The wind fanned the flames, which was good, but then Cockram felt the cold kiss of a raindrop on his cheek.

As he watched, a light sprinkle began to fall, dampening the reeds. His fire hissed and began to flag.

"No." Cockram whispered the word, a sense of horror creeping over him. Had he really come to this moment, invested his whole self at last, only to be crushed by a storm?

"No." He spoke with more certainty this time. He remembered that moment in the forest, and the one before that, facing the mob. He remembered that feeling – the well of energy inside him that could be scooped up and wielded.

He reached for the power, and felt it waiting. He felt a giddy rush of clarity. Finally, finally, he understood.

This was how he would win. He would use the piece of himself he'd denied his entire life. He would wield it as a weapon against its source.

Cockram pulled on his power, gathering it in, then flung it clumsily towards the flames. The fire flared, hissing, steam rising with smoke. He felt a moment of hope. But all too soon, the drizzle gained ground again.

Cockram reached for more power. He gritted his teeth and pulled for energy. His reserves were already drained, however. He was running on empty and his work hadn't even begun.

His hair was wet, plastered to his forehead and neck. Shivering, he stared at the dying fire. Surely, this would not be the end of his final battle?

He never knew what made him look down. Some sixth sense, perhaps. He felt a twinge of presence, and lowered his gaze to see a brinlin perched on the toe of his boot.

She was a brilliant shade of turquoise, with hot reds spots thrown across her vibrant hide. She looked up at him, and cheeped. The sound seemed to contain a question and an answer in one.

Rationally, Cockram knew he should shake her off, slap her away, stomp her small, soft body into the earth.

He did none of these things. Mesmerized, Cockram stooped. He extended his hand. She reached for him. He felt the soft grip of her delicate webbed feet as she climbed onto his finger.

The world dipped, swayed, and came back into focus. Cockram stood, his white shirt plastered to his chest, water running across his eye patch, and felt the strangest sense of shock.

A part of him that had been broken his whole life, a jagged end that had always hurt him, fused itself to this creature. The gap closed, the wound healed, and Cockram was whole for the first time in his life.

He was joined, now. To Mik. The brinlin's name was Mik.

And as that fusion happened, Cockram felt something else. Power. There was power in this animal, and in their bond. The small pool of magic Cockram had held in himself was a drop in a bucket compared to what he felt now.

Suddenly giddy with a renewed sense of triumph, Cockram opened his eyes and raised his hands. He understood so many things, now. Using his new power, he fanned the flames.

The fires caught with a whoosh, exploding into a towering inferno that stretched hot fingers into the sky and began to rush up the shore in both directions, towards the waiting forest.

☩

Marim was there, standing on the quay, when Vailria and Captain Tommin tied off to one of the old stone piers of Carreg Dinas. Rain had begun by then, a light drizzle. She shivered with some mix of actual cold and a strange sense of trepidation. They'd seen her from a ways out, they knew she was there. But they did not speak to her or acknowledge her presence until they'd disembarked and were walking together in her direction. Marim felt a brittle kaleidoscope of confused emotions. As they drew near, she could think of only one thing to say. "I thought you had returned to Masidon, Captain Tommin."

The man had the decency to grimace. "I'm no man's captain young miss. Not anymore. My ship is sold, my trading days done. There'll be another ship along to take you home, no doubt. Like that one yon."

He nodded towards the anchored Tessilari vessel that still sat in the middle of the cove. Marim could see the shapes of the sailors lined up on the rail, watching them through the light rain.

Vailria stood next to Tommin, arms crossed, expression remote. She wasn't looking at Marim, she was studying the cliffs above the harbor mouth. "I don't know how we're going to get up there, or even if that's where we need to go." She pulled her cloak in around her body and shivered. Her hair was wet, skin pale. She glanced to the south. "We don't have much time."

Kix, who'd been on the other side of his stitchring dozing in the warm sun in the greenhouse at Tessili Academy, woke as Marim's emotions intensified. He came bursting back through the ring to dart into the gray, chill air. The transportation spell dragged on Marim's reserves, making her momentarily woozy. She blinked and wiped rainwater out of her eyes. When she focused again, she saw both Vailria and Tommin watching her tessila with blended apprehension and dislike.

Vailria drew herself up a little taller, looking directly at Marim for the first time. "I don't have time for whatever vendetta you're carrying, Tessilar. Some magic has come awake here. It is wounded, and it has called up this storm. I need to warn Gol Ledrith."

As Marim felt her resentment for this woman flare all the higher, she saw Tommin's eyes flick to something behind her. She turned to see Jey, Treyam, and Coll walking out onto the docks.

The three drew up to join them. Looking at Coll, Marim's heart gave a strange clench. His face was sharp, his eyes intent and interested. He spoke in a calm, collected tone, as if he'd been part of the conversation from the beginning. "There's no one in Gol Ledrith. They've all headed for Lan Dinas. There's a magical fire in the reeds, heading for the forest. And also, you know, that." He jutted his chin towards the roiling black thunderhead still creeping towards the island at an inexorable crawl. His hood was up, beaded with rainwater. He spoke without a trace of uncertainty. "I can feel the break in the island's magic, but I don't know where it is. Jey and Treyam say they have to go back to the ship. They're afraid the storm will smash it to pieces if they don't shield it." He turned to Marim with an air of casual confidence. "So you and I are going to have to find the problem and fix it ourselves."

Marim looked at Treyam, who gave a small nod and turned to follow Jey, who was already unmooring their small boat from where they'd tied it to a pier. Marim looked back at Coll.

The sight of his glittering eyes brought a sharp, dense emotion to life in the pit of Marim's stomach. She wouldn't call it fear. She would never fear Coll—the boy she'd all but raised—who'd once needed her in a way no one else in Marim's life ever had. He looked at her now, his mouth turned up in the barest hint of a smile. "Where's your beau run off to? He'd be useful to have along."

The comment brought heat to Marim's cheeks. She knew Coll too well, knew he was trying to bait her.

Ignoring the comment, Marim looked at Vailria. The woman seemed to be weighing her options, taking the measure of Coll and Marim and the coming storm. As Jey and Treyam cast off, rowing towards the bucking ship, the rain picked up and a distant rumble of thunder sounded from over the water. She seemed to come to a decision. "There's a light in the sky above the summit. It shifts and sizzles, flickering – on and off, the magic stuttering in and out of it. It's been drawing the clouds in all day, and they gather around the peak now. I could see it from our island across the channel, so we came back. We came to help."

This last, she directed to no one in particular, but Marim felt it was targeted at her, as if she was trying to imply this noble act made up for the way she'd abandoned Marim on the docks with a murderous man at her heels.

As Coll raised his eyes to look at the cliffs that surrounded the cove, Marim pushed all her hurt and confusion aside. Tommin had retraced his steps to the small vessel that was lurching and dancing on the chop. He returned with a length of soft, white rope coiled about his shoulder. As he joined them again, he gave it a pat and winked at Marim. "You never know when a good rope can save the day."

Coll was still staring up at the mountain, eyes narrow, hood dripping water. But Marim was thinking of the carved benches on the summit where she and Braven and Tassin had taken a break from their climb that seemed so long ago now. She thought of the high point of the island, the cracked globe, and the runes. The thought of the day she'd opened the mountain, the way the sparks had leapt up out of the broken pillar and the damaged globe above the door.

"The summit," she said. "There's a giant globe there, cracked down the middle. If power has got into it again, it will be causing problems. But it's a long way up the top of the island, and steep."

Coll was eyeing Tommin's rope. "Wip could carry a person if she had some sort of harness," he said. "She couldn't fly in this. Not safely. But she can climb very quickly."

Embriem had woken from a disorienting bad dream into a nightmare. As he sat with the kindly old Brinlock who explained to him what had happened, parceling out the details in small pieces to make sure Embriem could handle the information, he saw the shower of red sparks burst into the sky as the shadow of a great storm fell across the city. He heard the eerie ring of the great gong. He saw the Brinlocks gather in the square at the heart of Gol Ledrith, heard Aldrath's booming voice, amplified by some spell. The Brinlock was addressing the crowd to explain that Lan Dinas was in peril.

According to Aldrath, the harbor town was usually safe enough from storms. The violent systems always came from the northwest, and they broke against the island's rocky side, spending their lightning and ferocious winds on the uncaring cliffs and jagged peaks that ringed the north and west shores.

This storm was different. Approaching from the south, it would hit Lan Dinas first. The storm would enrage the sea, calling up great waves to crash and batter. Lightning might cause fires. The streets would flood, buildings would shatter. There would be great loss of life.

It was time, Aldrath said, for the Brinlocks to come out of hiding. Fate had delivered this opportunity. The Guardians and the Keepers would emerge now and stand against the storm as an act of good will the people of Lan Dinas could witness and appreciate. They would protect the city, and use their magics to shield the people until the storm spent itself and moved on. It would be the beginning of a new era in which Gol Ledrith and Lan Dinas existed in partnership.

The speech was stirring. Aldrath called upon his brethren to set aside their fear, to see this as an opportunity to earn a hero's welcome and sidestep the social backlash they'd feared for generations. He said the time for hiding was over, one way or another, and they must embrace change.

Embriem heard all this from within his apartment, after the healer left. She'd allowed him to open a window. He'd listened to the rise and fall of the words while he sat with Nel, who was ecstatic with joy but also so weak and thin it hurt Embriem to look at her.

It was about this time a runner burst into the square, pushed through to Aldrath, and announced the woods were on fire. There was a collective gasp, murmurs of confusion and horror. The crowd swayed like a net full of fish, quivering with a need to be set free. Aldrath addressed them with a few final words. "Keepers, with me. We will go to Lan Dinas and shelter the city from the storm. Guardians and the rest of you Brinlocks that would save our island, to the forest to fight the flames."

It took mere minutes for the square to empty. Anyone who might have chosen to stay behind was hidden – skulking behind walls.

Embriem sat listening to the light patter of rain on the roof, looking down at his bony wrists, his thin hands. The healer had explained there'd been a spell on him. It had caused him to think and feel things he wouldn't normally think and feel. He tried to remember what those things might have been, but the recent past was shrouded in his mind. His last clear memory was of Marim, grabbing his wrist and saying, "Come with me."

There was the click of a latch. The door to Tassin's room opened, and Embriem's son emerged. Embriem stared at him, shocked. He was so sturdy, so healthy. He looked as if he'd sprouted several inches sand gained a stone since Embriem had last clapped eyes on him.

Embriem surged to his feet, emotion choking his throat. "Tassin. They told me you were out, down in the city with your mentor."

Tassin was wearing a cloak. Water dripped from its hem onto the floor. His light hair was wet with rain. He brought the smell of the storm with him. "It's true then?" His voice was cautious, his expression skeptical. "You're better? Really better?"

Nel climbed up Embriem's collar and swiveled her head towards Tassin, letting out a soft, glad peep. The boy smiled then. For a moment, Embriem thought he would run across the room, wrap his arms around his waist like he used to do when he was small.

But something held him back, and something kept Embriem from taking a step forward. "Yes, they say I'm better. Although the door is still locked."

Tassin's mouth twitched into a smile. "That's why I came in through my room. I've picked the lock on the balcony doors. We can get out that way without being seen. I'm going back to Lan Dinas. We're the only people who know both sides, who can work to convince our old friends and family the Brinlocks are not our enemy. You can come, if you want."

Embriem's first reaction was one of fear. He straightened up, trying to inject authority into his voice. "You're not doing any such thing. It's far too dangerous. Tassin, get back here."

As Embriem spoke, Tassin backed away, moving one step at a time closer to the open door that led into his bedroom. There was only one lamp in the room. It threw long shadows that made his son look like a stranger. When had he grown so tall?

"I'm going, one way or another." Tassin's words were firm, his voice unwavering. "I hoped you'd want to come, too, but I've been studying the magics of the Brinlocks for nine months, father. You can't stop me going."

CHAPTER 6

Fog and smoke mixed with rain. A chill wind lashed across Braven's face. Cold, nervous, and more than a little uncertain, Braven piloted his light craft down the river, pushing on the spell that made the boat quick and light to pour on even more speed.

Around him, other Brinlocks hunched over their oars. Ahead, he saw the orange glow of the fire. As he paddled around a bend in the river, he went still with horror and amazement. Where the river ended in the lake, the reeds and trees were all ablaze. Bright licks of flame stretched up towards the crowns of the towering trees, and the air was thick with smoke.

Braven's shock and fear held him immobile for a moment. How was it possible? With the rain, no fire should have been able to spread like this, to grow so fierce and tall. The reeds were alive. The trees were alive. The woodcutters saw there was very little deadwood about. Why was this fire burning so bright and so fast?

Behind him, Aldrath's voice boomed from his own vessel. "Cast a passive barrier spell, and push through. Remember, we go to the city. Don't let the fire distract you from your mission."

Abruptly, Braven realized how quickly he was still moving. The magic of the boat was awake and lively, fueled by the extra power he'd been feeding into its weave. The air around him had gone dry and crackly. Ash sifted down from burning branches, along with falling sparks. His lungs filled with heat and smoke and the sweet smell of boiling sap.

Braven grasped at his magic, wove his spell, and released. He took care to shelter the boat as well as himself, and reach as far as he could to help shield the Brinlocks behind him. Then he poured more power into his boat, and the craft gained speed. It bore down on the wall of fire that was the burning reeds. For a moment, his eyes searched frantically for the break that must be there, when the river widened into the lake.

He couldn't see it. For one horrible moment, he thought the current would deliver him straight into an inferno.

Then, he was through. His boat rushed around a final bend and shot between two leaping walls of flame. He felt the heat even through his shield and had to close his eyes against the glare. But then he was past, through, safe. The burning banks fell away on either side, and he was out on the surface of the quiet warmlake. His boat skimmed along at a good clip, heading for the far shore.

Above, lightning forked across the sky. As the fire fell behind, Braven became aware of the mass of the storm – its frantic, roiling magic. He did not let the craft slow.

Landing was easier than usual. As he reached the end of the lake closest to Lan Dinas, he did not have to look for a spit of sand or a hiding place among the reeds. The reeds were gone – burned down to black stubs. As he paddled up the shore, he realized with a sick feeling of disbelief that the fire had started here, close to town, only to spread all the way along the lake to reach the forest at last.

As he understood this, Braven felt a twinge of desire to go back, to defend his beloved woods instead of these people – these selfish people who tried to chop down sacred trees and murdered their own children just for showing an aptitude for magics. Why should the Brinlocks care if the lightning cracked their houses, leaving fire and death behind? Why should the Brinlocks care if the sea smashed the harbor and spilled into the streets, bringing cold death to anyone who couldn't find higher ground?

Aldrath said it was time to come out of hiding, but Braven didn't see why. They could hold the forest. They could hold the cove. If they let this storm wreck Lan Dinas, they could drive the last of its people away in the days and weeks and months to come. They could have the entire island, the entire warmlake, to themselves.

Thinking these thoughts, Braven ran his ship aground, staring at the smoking stumps of burnt off reeds. He felt a surge of fear for the brinlins. They could stay in water for a long time, but they could not swim indefinitely. With no reeds to perch on, would they die?

He sat in his boat for a moment, quivering and undecided, until Aldrath's voice boomed through the smoke and rain. "Brinlocks, form up on the beach. Each of you exchange a thread with two others, and one with me. Then, spread out. We'll form a circle around the town and throw up a spell to shield the buildings and the people from the storm. We have only to hold until the worst of the system passes."

With a twist of regret, Braven hopped into the shallows and dragged his boat onto the charred shore. He could not leave his fellow Keepers to fight the storm without him. Still, as he listened to Aldrath's words, a strange thought squirmed into his mind. *The storm isn't going to pass. Not this one. It will batter us until we're exhausted, then rip the city apart in spite of our efforts.*

It was such a strange, bleak though, Braven found himself momentarily arrested.

All storms passed. Why would this one be any different?

The streets of Lan Dinas were deserted – the people of the city having apparently more sense than the Brinlocks Aldrath had led through an inferno to defend this city that wasn't even theirs.

Aldrath stood with his eyes closed, hearing the drum of the frigid rain on his drawn up hood. He alone stood in the town square at the center of the web of threadlines that connected all his Keepers. He held each one in his mind, nudging here, tugging there, until, at last, all his people were in position.

Around him, lights burned in windows, but the town was silent. Not a soul had so far ventured into the square to inquire what this strange man might be doing. He hoped, at least, the people were watching through their windows. Heroes needed their good deeds witnessed.

When all his Brinlocks had settled, their threadlines going still, Aldrath sent a thought out so it slithered up every line and reached the mage on the other end. *Together now. Raise a passive calming spell and pass a grip to me.*

Lightning crashed and shuddered in the sky. There was a crack and a roar as a building a few blocks away burst into flame. There were screams and shouts and the sudden ringing of a bell. Aldrath pushed it all out of his mind. Surely the people here could put out one fire. He needed to make sure no more started.

One by one, the frayed edges of spells were offered to him, stretched thin as they were pushed across the space between him and his mages.

He accepted them as they came, and reached out to knit each weave together, running his mind along the edges to bind consecutive spells together into one great dome of magic. With each new piece, the strength of the entire creation grew. He felt a few other minds at work, helping bind their own spells with their neighbors' and lending strength to the entire structure. That was as it should be. The strong gave all they could. The weaker casters focused simply on holding their own.

In the air above Lan Dinas, the air began to shiver. The spell grew visible as it took shape. Aldrath, at its hub, united the last of the weaves with a sense of satisfaction, then added his own power to the completed spell. He looked up at the great, shimmering protective dome now arching over the city.

On the other side of the magic, the storm grew wilder. But quiet fell over the square. The rain reduced to a fine mist. Shutters that had been banging in the fitful wind fell quiet. When thunder roared overheard, the sound was muffled.

Satisfied, Aldrath lowered his eyes to the streets once more. That's when he saw he was no longer alone.

A woman stood before him. She was tall and straight, with narrow shoulders and sharp eyes. She wore a cloak with the hood drawn up, leaving some of her face in shadow. She spoke in a quiet, measured tone. "You came out of the forest." It wasn't a question.

Aldrath had only a small amount of attention to spare. The storm was growing more violent by the moment. Even as she spoke, a hissing bolt of lightning cracked into the passive calming spell. It sent slithering, dancing light snaking across the dome. Aldrath felt the strain, but the spell held. "Yes." He caught a better glimpse of the woman's face as the air lit. He saw a slender neck and a long fall of dark hair.

She turned towards the lake. Even from this distance, the sky over the forest was smudged with angry red. "My father is like you." Her words were low and urgent, and she took a step closer. "Only he's gone mad, I think. He's the one making the fire so hot. I followed him. I saw him on the lake shore. I watched him drive the flames faster and faster until they reached the trees."

Lightning hit the shield again, stronger this time. Aldrath grunted with the impact, feeling it like a stone against his temple. He closed his eyes again, aware the woman was still talking but with no attention to spare. Lightning struck again, and again. He heard it crack, felt the blows. His feeling of satisfaction began to fade. Some of the Brinlocks were fading already, their sections of the weave growing weak.

Aldrath sent his mind up into the spell, pouring in all the power he had to spare.

As he lifted his awareness, he brushed against the storm. And he felt something that filled his heart with terror.

The storm was no longer moving. It had settled over them like a cloud of flies over a corpse. As he groped up into the sky, he felt it was tethered to the island by a rope of thick, inky magic.

Much too late, Aldrath understood.

The storm wasn't a freak occurrence, a once in an era's event. It had been caused and called by the broken magic on this island. It wasn't going to pass, no matter how long his Brinlocks held this shield.

Unless, he thought, it could be broken apart: blown to bits from the inside.

Gently, Aldrath disentangled himself from the passive calming spell. The rest of the Brinlocks would have to hold it without him. Eyes still closed he focused, gathering all his remaining power to bear.

He'd forgotten about the woman. He didn't hear her when she said, "He must be stopped. Someone has to stop him." He didn't notice the way she stood for a few more moments, watching him, waiting. He didn't see the resolve that hardened in her eyes just before she squared her shoulders and moved off, heading out of the square, towards the warmlake.

Aldrath wove a spell he had no name for, reaching into the storm and feeling its rage. He understood something as he worked. The Tessilari might have more ability to wield raw, aggressive magics. Tessili might be able to fly and shift and kill. But where a Tessilari fought, a Brinlock influenced. Where a tessila beat against the wind, a brinlin moved with the current. Aldrath knew he could not fight the storm, but he could use its own power against it and turn it into something a good deal less harmful.

Alone in the square, Aldrath wove the largest, most intricate spell of his life. As the first section of shield gave way to a lightning strike, he opened his eyes, and released.

Wip was huge again. She was massive and scaly and her talons could bite into stone. Tommin's rope was snugged around her shoulders, tied off to give a person sitting astride her broad back something to grip. One by one, she'd carried them up the mountain, scrabbling up sheer slopes, using her wings to propel herself over perilous terrain. The ride was hair-raising and stomach twisting. Once Marim was left at the top, she couldn't help but goggle at the massive animal every time she lunged over the ledge by the stone circle with its benches to drop off another passenger.

At last, Wip made her final climb. When she reached the summit, Coll swung down from her shoulder. Vailria was holding some kind of elastic shield around them all, protecting the stone circle from the worst of the storm. Above and ahead, the summit of Cynnes Tarth loomed in the murky air – a ragged shadow that spit fitful showers of sparks at random intervals.

The storm was fierce, but Marim got the idea it was more violent near the coast. Fully three quarters of the island was ringed in cliffs that could sustain a beating from the violent sea. Only two places were vulnerable to such weather. The cove, where the Tessilari ship stood at anchor, and the coast upon which Lan Dinas was built. Gol Ledrith, far inland, surrounded by massive trees and sheltering mountains, was safe.

At least, that was what Marim had thought. Looking down now, she could see a smear of red and orange in the sky. Was the forest burning? Lightning cracked off the surrounding peaks, and far below, in the hidden cove, the anchored ship rocked and swayed while Jey and Treyam did whatever they could to defend it from the storm.

Vailria, seeing the direction of Marim's gaze, spoke in a cool tone of authority. "We can't worry about that now. Our task is here. Show me this broken globe."

Marim pointed. The storm obliged by flinging lightning across the entire sky. In the flash of light, the peak loomed. For an instant, the globe was visible, a luminous shape nestled against the overhanging stone. A restless light seemed to flicker within its depths. As they stared, sparks burst out of the crack, leaping into the sky and turning red as they flew.

Vailria seemed to lose some of her confidence, and Marim could see why. Between where they stood among the stone benches and the peak, there was only the jagged spine of the mountain. To reach the globe, a person would have to make a steep climb with a sheer drop on either side.

Marim felt a twinge of unease. "I wonder if we could repair it from here."

Vailria turned to her with a look of hooded scorn. "Of course we can't. The manipulation of physical matter requires a point of contact. I thought you went to an academy of magics."

Heat rushed to Marim's cheeks. She'd forgotten how caustic this woman could be. For an instant, she thought of taking Coll and leaving, riding Wip down and letting Vailria deal with this problem on her own.

But she thought of the bucking vessel in the harbor – her ticket home. If this storm came and stayed, like Vailria said it was going to, Jey and Treyam would eventually exhaust themselves. The ship would sink and no other would come.

Don't rise to the bait, she told herself. She glanced at Coll, who was standing and staring at the globe with a set in his shoulders Marim recognized all too well. She'd seen him like this as a boy. He only looked this way when he'd decided on a course of action, usually an ill-thought out one, and was about to do something foolish.

Before Marim could speak up, before she could try to break into his thoughts and redirect them, Coll turned around. A gust of wind broke through Vailria's shield and tugged at his cloak, which he took off and tossed to the ground by one of the benches. "Wip will carry me out. Vailria, can you extend your shield far enough to cover me?"

In Vailria's face, Marim could see the answer was no. The woman's lips tightened. "I should be the one to repair the globe. It's brinlin magic that forged these great works."

But Coll was turning away. He was in no mood for listening. "Wip won't leave me back here in this storm, and a person alone would get blown straight off the cliff."

As Coll turned back to heave himself onto Wip's back, Marim found her voice at last. "Coll. No. It's too dangerous. Let Vailria. Let me."

She might as well not have spoken. Her words had less impact on the young man than the mist. He settled onto Wip's rain-slicked shoulders, knotted his hands in the rope, and gave her a pat on the neck. The tessila scuttled away, wings tucked, holding her body low to give the wind less to grab. Still, when she pushed past Vailria's shield, the wind almost tore her free of the cliff. The massive animal hunched, talons biting into stone as she held onto the mountain and Coll held onto her.

Without thinking, Marim reached out and snatched Vailria's hand. The other woman gave a gasp and a jerk, trying to pull free. But Marim didn't let go. Instead, she felt for the shield spell, found it, and dumped magic into the weaving in a frantic rush.

Vailria's eyes went wide. She stopped pulling against Marim's grip. She blinked twice, and the shield widened, pushing out past the benches, past Wip, and finally, past the peak of Cynnes Tarth itself.

As the lashing wind died to fitful gusts, Coll turned around, saw Marim holding Vailria's hand, and gave her one of his grins. It was an expression of pure excitement and happiness. "He loves attempting the impossible." Marim said this by way of explanation.

Vailria's hand was wet and cold in Marim's grip. Her tone was grudging. "He's going to get himself killed."

But Marim didn't think so. Not as long as they could hold their shield. She herself felt full of energy, plenty strong to keep the weave in place for a good while.

In a moment, Coll had reached the globe. He slid down from his Tessila, keeping one hand gripped to Tommin's rope while he set the other on the globe.

It was Tommin who warned Marim what was coming. "Vailria," the sailor said, tone tense. Marim turned to see the man step forward as Vailria, face pale, slumped to one side. Marim felt the passive calming spell flag. Cold rain slashed across her face. Frantic, she poured more of her own energy into the spell. But Vailria's eyes were fluttering. She was exhausted, Marim realized, and losing consciousness.

"She called up a wind that blew us before the storm the whole way over," Tommin said. "I told her it was too much, she'd do herself harm. But she said we'd come to more harm if the storm caught us."

Horrified, Marim felt the spell's weave come apart. She tried to seize the threads, tried to hold them together, but she couldn't force her magic into the right pattern. This is how Embriem must have felt, she thought, when she tried to teach him a simple active strike spell. It was as impossible as trying to walk on water. Her magic couldn't take the right shape.

As the spell unraveled, Marim turned, heart in her throat, just in time to see Coll tumble off the mountain.

The forest was burning. The air was hot and choked with smoke. Ferns blazed like torches. Leaves hissed as flames consumed them. The flames were even licking against the great trunks, trying to catch hold.

The forest was burning, and it was Adni's fault. Yesterday, she'd had two chances to see her brother die. She could have let him fall before the Tessilari, or she could have killed him herself.

She'd done neither of these things. Instead, she'd thrown her arm around his shoulders and hidden him from the Tessilari boy who stalked like a dire through the trees. She'd led him out of the forest, back to his pub. She'd muddled his mind with a passive persuasion spell, put him to bed, and left. Afterwards, she hadn't returned to Gol Ledrith, to her own quiet home on the lake. She'd gone instead to a small house on the outskirts of Lan Dinas. It was abandoned now, with a roof that needed rereeding and a boarded up window in front. It had been unoccupied since Adni's mother died some years before.

The house hadn't been emptied. She supposed it belonged to Cockram, and he'd not bothered with selling it. The door was locked, but Adni made quick work of that. When she'd walked across the threshold, it had been like going back in time.

The kitchen and dining area were as she remembered, with the short, dark hall leading back towards the bedrooms. She groped along the wall as she went, turned left, and set her fingers on a closed door.

It creaked as she pushed, swinging inwards to reveal a small bedroom. It was a plain space, with a single bed pushed against one wall and a chair in the corner.

That was it. There was no sign of any toys or belongings the girl who'd grown up sleeping between these four walls had once loved.

To Adni, the room felt small and airless. She walked to the bed, staring at the faded walls, and sat down. She lay back on the reed stuffed ticking, smelling dust, and stared up at the cracked plaster of the ceiling. Her childhood had not been so bad, she thought. She and Cockram had been close, in their own way. Their parents had loved them, even if they hadn't had much to give by way of material support.

Lying in her old bedroom, listening to the creak of the wind in the eaves, Adni wondered if she'd been wrong all these years. She'd thought she wanted revenge. She'd dreamed of all the ways she could make Cockram pay for what he'd done. She'd wanted to make him bitterly regret the way he'd wronged her, and then watch him die.

Now, she didn't know if she could follow through. It was no surprise, really. He'd always been made of sterner stuff than she, always better able to do what he was told. Adni had never been able to resist the warmlake. She'd never wasted a chance to slip away and play in the shallows. She knew it called to him the same way it had her. Yet he'd fought the pull all his life, because he believed the power of the brinlins was evil.

In her old bedroom, in her old bed, Adni had fallen asleep. She'd slept through the night, into the day, and been awakened by thunder. Disoriented, cold, hungry, she'd gone outside. Stepping into the cold rain, closing the house's door behind her, she'd turned to see the lurid, smoke-filled sky.

She'd walked down to the lake shore as a massive spell was raised up over Lan Dinas. She'd skirted the Brinlocks she saw on the outskirts of town, feeling disoriented by their open presence here. Had she slept a century instead of a night?

She'd gone to the lake, where she'd found Tilde, her niece, standing among the stumps of burnt reeds.

Turning, Tilde seemed to take Adni in: the shifting cloak, the lines of her face. The two had never met, but that didn't seem to matter. Tilde spoke in a low, tired tone. "I always wondered if you really died."

Too surprised to say anything, too shocked by the sight of the reedless shore, Adni only stared. Tilde went on, gesturing at the denuded lake. "It's him. He's gone mad. He came down here, set this fire. Now he's feeding it somehow. We have to stop him."

Adni shook her head, turning to gaze towards the burning forest. "I have to stop him. You have to stay here. Stay safe."

Tilde looked at the water of the warmlake, her face tight with concern. "They'll die won't they? Without the reeds?"

At first, Adni didn't know what she meant. Then she saw the brinlins, swirling and colorful, moving in schools beneath the surface of the lake. Some had crawled out of the water onto blackened stumps of reeds, others were hauling their ill-suited bodies onto the sand.

It was true. The animals needed to breathe, to rest. They would tire and die with no reeds to climb upon.

Lightning flickered and boomed. The sky was so dark, it seemed like midnight. Adni gave a short, tight nod.

Tilde ran a hand over her damp, wind-tossed hair and glanced back towards the town. "We have plenty of reeds at the pub. Bundles and bundles. I'll bring them down here, set them loose on the water. They'll float, right? And the brinlins can climb up and rest?"

It would take every stored reed in all of Lan Dinas to save every brinlin in the lake, but Adni didn't have the heart to puncture the girl's resolve. She only nodded. "I have to go."

Tilde lifted her face then. Adni thought at first it was rain on her face, but then the girl drew in a shuddering breath. "If you can stop him without killing him ..."

She hadn't finished the sentence, and Adni hadn't answered. She'd clasped her niece's hand, and hurried away.

Now she was in the woods, walking through the blaze, her gut clenched with horror. Around her, she was aware of Brinlocks working against the fire, organized in lines to break the blaze's progress and push it back towards the lake. She was aware, also, of another force – someone flinging power at the fire, pushing it inland, towards Gol Ledrith.

Later, Adni would always tell herself it couldn't have ended any other way. By the time she found her brother, he had turned into a madman. He strode among the burning trees, a brinlin clinging to his sleeve. He knew no spellwork, but he was powerful and intuitive. The fire responded to his wild weavings, burning like a thing possessed.

Cockram's white shirt was gray with ash. His eye patch was gone, leaving the ruin of his eye exposed. His remaining eye glittered with hate and glee as he turned to watch a massive branch, all ablaze, crash down and hit the lake waters, where it began to steam.

It took a moment to sink in, for Adni to accept the evidence before her eyes.

After all these years, Cockram had given in at last. He'd succumbed to the lake's call.

For a moment, Adni felt her heart lift with hope. The bonding process could be disorienting, particularly when it happened late in life. All her brother needed was some time, some education. He was confused right now, and naturally thrown off balance. He only needed a little guidance.

Adni hurried a few steps forward, stepping around the trunk of a tree that was beginning to seep steam into the parched air. Cockram turned, saw her, and went still.

She was about to call his name, to rush forward, when the gleam in his eye made her go still. He glared at her through the hot air, his face creased with hate. "You," he bellowed. "This all because of you." He flung a hand outwards to encompass the burnings woods, the roiling sky, the lost years between them.

It didn't matter that he was wrong, that if you traced the thread of the story back to its origins, it was the deceased rector who'd started the war between them. There was no time to convince him, to try to change his mind.

Her brother reached out, heaved on his magic, and Adni's cloak burst into flame. As she wove a counter-spell to dampen the fire, Cockram drew a knife from his belt, and charged.

As her brother ran towards her with murder in his eyes, Adni felt he was already over-extended. Dozens of spells were tied to him, drawing on his reserves. He didn't understand the risks of impulsive, intuitive casting. He knew nothing about the power he wielded. Adni could feel the way those spells dragged on him, pulling draining, consuming.

Every now and then, it happened this way. A Brinlock became a Brinlock only to go drunk on his new power and expend his own life in an orgy of casting.

It would have happened, one way or another. If Adni had not sidestepped the charge and used one end of her staff to trip Cockram, then brought the other end down across the base of his skull as he fell, he still would have died that day. Running from the inevitable would only have let him do more damage—wreak a few more minutes of destruction—only to die anyway.

Adni knew her weapon, knew her mark, knew her art. The first blow was a killing one, but she followed up with a second, just to be sure.

Then she stood still, lungs burning with smoke, eyes streaming with tears.

One by one, the fires around her began to go out.

CHAPTER 7

A scream burst past Marim's lips, jerked from her like a hooked fish pulled from the sea. "No! Coll!"

But it was too late. His body tumbled, spun, and fell out of sight. Wip, quick as a striking snake, released her grip on the mountain and dove after him.

Marim stood, heart pounding, wet to the skin and only half aware of Tommin lowering Vailria to the ground and pressing his hand against her forehead as if feeling for fever. Marim stared at the cracked globe as the wind shook her. Sparks leapt, and lightning seared the sky.

It was over. They'd failed, and Coll had paid with his life. They would all die here, exposed on the mountain, defenseless against this terrible storm.

Kix, who did not like the cold rain, let out a strange, sad cry. Marim continued to stare into gloom, unwilling to believe. If Coll's body smashed on the stones below, so too would Wip die. Would the tessila's body shrink upon her death, Marim wondered?

Or would it fall in all its glorious bulk, a massive testament to Coll's wasted potential?

Despair settled over her like an iron curtain. She'd hurt so many people with her mistakes, but not Coll. Never Coll.

Until now.

She stared at the shifting fog, at the open air off the side of the mountain. *If I die, I cannot hurt anyone else.*

"Marim."

She ignored the voice. It was too late to change anything, and she knew she could not live with this final error. If she'd never come to the Fog Isles, Coll wouldn't have either. If she'd never repaired that pillar, he never would have been on this mountain in a magical storm.

Yes. Best she die.

She took a step towards the edge.

A firm hand fell on her shoulder. She turned, startled. Tommin stood behind her, his expression grave and firm. "What can you do for her? Her pulse is weak. Once, when you wanted passage off the mainland, you said you were good at healing. Was that true?"

Marim wanted to shrug out from under his hand, to abandon him the way he'd once abandoned her, to wrench herself free and tumble triumphantly to her doom. What reason did she have to save Vailria, a woman who had only ever looked out for herself?

But looking at Tommin's wet beard, his red eyes, Marim felt the grip of despair on her heart loosen a little. She remembered him on his ship, when she'd made a mistake and seemingly consigned herself, him, and his entire crew to death. He hadn't blamed or punished or raged. Maybe she could do this one bit of good before she went.

She gave a small nod. "I'll try."

She was about to kneel, to set her hand on Vailria again, when she saw a blur of movement that made her look back towards the cracked globe.

It was a great black wing, rising and falling. Marim strained downwards to see Wip, Coll clutched in her talons, fighting up against the vicious wind. As Marim watched, she gained altitude inch by painstaking inch. She couldn't climb, Marim realized, without smashing Coll into the cliffs.

How to help? Marim couldn't think of a way. She felt frozen, helpless, powerless and chilled.

She was still staring, still uncertain, when the sky exploded.

Later, of course, Marim would learn of Aldrath's spell – the massive effort the Brinlock expended in an attempt to shatter the storm, break its connection to the island, and save Lan Dinas. She would learn how he collapsed in a heap on the stones of the town square, and how the same newly minted Brinlock named Tilde saved his life when he would have died from over-extension with a purely intuitive spell of passive replenishment, then went on to rally the town to return bundle upon bundle of harvested reeds to the warmlake so thousands of brinlins would not drown for lack of somewhere to perch.

Aldrath's spell, despite its enormous power and cost, would fail in its objective. It did not unravel the storm, as Aldrath intended. But it did suspend its activity for a short time.

At that moment, as Marim stood on the mountain staring up at the blasted sky, she did not know what was happening below. She had no way of guessing if the light in the sky was a good a sign, or a terrible one. She only knew the storm seemed to shudder to a stop. The wind died, the lightning ceased, and the whole island was momentarily wrapped in glowing, suspended calm.

Wip, pushing suddenly against nothing, wheeled upwards in a sudden burst of altitude, then swooped back down, deposited Coll by the cracked globe, and resumed her crouched position so he could once again grip her improved harness while he knelt to touch the polished stone of the cracked orb.

Marim's heart was in her throat. She couldn't believe he would try again after such a near miss. Overhead, the sky seemed to buckle and flame. Light rippled and snaked through the thunderheads in their strange shape. "Marim." Tommin spoke her name again, his tone urgent. "Please. You can't help him, but you can help her."

With reluctance, Marim tore her eyes away from Coll. She knelt by Vailria, touching the woman's cold hand. She let a thread of her own magic snake into Vailria.

The Brinlock was exhausted, her reserves all but gone. Marim felt at her own reserves, and was surprised to find them nearly undiminished. So she worked a weaving she'd learned ages ago, at the academy: a spell of active replenishment.

As Marim released her weave, color bloomed back into Vailria's face. The woman's eyes flicked open.

Around them, a fitful wind fingered Marim's wet hair. The sky began to lose its glow. Their moment's reprieve was nearly spent.

Marim looked up. Coll still knelt by the globe, Wip crouched beside him, wings spread low in a defensive pose. The globe was glowing with a bright light.

How much longer did he need? How much longer did they have before the wind hit again? Marim didn't know either answer, but she didn't want to trust in fate for the equation to come out in their favor.

She spoke with urgency. "Vailria, weave your passive calming spell again. Make it small, tiny even. Don't worry about giving it power. Just weave it, and hold on. I will provide the power."

Tommin spoke, a feeble protest, but Marim ignored him. Vailria's eyes were sharp in her drawn face. They met Marim's and held. The woman nodded.

The next moment seemed to last an eternity. Above them, the sky faded to black. Lightning began to crash and boom again. Wip released a long low snarl as Coll was buffeted, nearly lost his footing, and righted himself only just in time. Vailria began her spell, and Marim waited, seething with impatience until she realized in a sudden flash of intuition that she could weave *with*

Vailria. She didn't have to wait until the spell was complete, then try to amplify it. She could lay her own lines of magic in among Vailria's, like a vine growing around a lattice.

She tried. As she let her magic flow, the passive calming spell burst into existence. It was the same as before, only larger, stronger, brighter, and more dynamic. As the storm rebounded from its temporary pause, the summit of Cynnes Tarth began to glow with two separate lights. One from the spell that kept the wind and lightning at bay, and one from the spell that bloomed beneath the palm of a teenage Tessilari as he repaired the cracked globe.

There was not so much as even a breeze. No mist of rain. Marim, Vailria, and Tommin waited in utter calm and watched as the stone beneath Coll's hand seemed to grow molten with white light. Marim could see the fissure in its surface. She watched as it smoothed over, filled in, and was gone.

The light faded. Coll tried to stand, wobbled, and fell to his knees. With an annoyed huff, Wip grabbed him in her talons again, flew the short distance through the still air to where the others waited, and dumped him by one of the benches. Then she flickered and seemed to disappear. Tommin's rope tumbled, empty, to the ground. Wip, no longer even as long as Marim's finger, flew down to bury herself in Coll's collar.

Above them, the storm unspun. Within a few heartbeats, the dark clouds began to tear like tissue, snags of blue sky showing through the murk.

Coll picked himself up. Marim turned in alarm as he released a strange series of gasping croaks. She was about to let go of Vailria and rush to his aid when she realized he was laughing. He was laughing so hard he was all but choking on dry heaves that sounded like sobs. "This," he said, wiping tears away from his eyes, "is the best day of my life."

Later, Marim would sometimes think back on this moment and wonder what he meant, exactly. At the time, she thought it was because he'd repaired the globe, untethered the storm, and saved Lan Dinas. Sometimes, though, in years to come, she would doubt that conclusion.

It was the challenge, she would come to believe in time – the near death, the possibility of becoming a martyr, the chance to display his considerable power and talent.

Coll liked being a hero.

In that moment, however, Marim was too spent to do much more than shake her head, look up into the sky, and watch the storm come undone.

Embriem stood just inside his large house, the door still open behind him, staring into the spacious hall. Miraculously, his property was undamaged. During his long absence, Tassin's two grandmothers had kept the place up in hopes the missing boy and his father would someday return.

In the coming days, Embriem would have a lot of explaining to do. He would have to explain to his mother why he and Tassin needed to leave – why they must move to Gol Ledrith in order to be always near their brinlins. Tassin needed to attend one of the schools of magics, and Embriem, too, needed to finally devote himself to understanding Nel and his bond with her.

Down below, in the city square, Aldrath and the mayor of Lan Dinas were addressing the populace. They were explaining how the deadly storm had settled over the island and would have maddened the ocean until it broke Lan Dinas to bits. The Brinlocks had come out of hiding to save the city.

It wasn't news to anyone. As the storm had begun to break up, Embriem and Tassin had finished their journey down the river. They'd passed through woods where fires blazed, choking on smoke until they reached the lake, only to arrive at a shore where reeds no longer grew. Embriem had felt dismayed as he and Tassin had hauled their stolen boat out of the water and hurried towards the city under its great dome of magic, believing they'd arrived too late to help. The storm was breaking up, sunlight beginning to crack through the clouds.

But Tassin had run through the streets, shouting that the Brinlocks had saved the city, and now the people of Lan Dinas needed to save the forest.

Normally, one small boy's words would not have had much of an impact. But Tassin was turning out to have a particular talent for atmospheric emotional casting. He released threads of curiosity and interest into the air as he ran, generating interest and sympathy and gratitude as he moved. It wasn't anything so concrete as persuasion. It was a strategic blend of subtle amplifiers that made people peek out from behind closed shutters, crack open doors, and step out into the slackening rain.

It took two days to contain the fires. Two days during which Brinlock and citizen of Lan Dinas stood shoulder to shoulder, one wielding a bucket, the other a staff.

By the time the forest was safe, everyone was exhausted. But friendships had formed. A tentative peace had been planted in the ashes of ferns and fallen leaves.

Gol Ledrith was no longer a secret. The forest was no longer a place of terrors, out of bounds and off limits. There was talk of a road, of docks to be built on the warmlake to encourage commerce and traffic between the two cities of Cynnes Tarth.

It was good news: tremendous progress. When Embriem and Tassin had returned home at last, they'd been greeted in the streets by old friends who hadn't spoken to them in months. It was as if the slow decline of Embriem's position had been reversed overnight. Now everyone in Lan Dinas wanted to be able to claim the friendship of a Brinlock.

In his office stood a stack of letters – new correspondence from the business contacts who had systematically frozen him out of their dealings only a scant few months before. Embriem could resume his life here, if he wanted.

Except, he found he did not want that. What he wanted was Tassin, Nel, and a quiet life in Gol Ledrith.

He would miss this house, though. Letting go was like saying goodbye to Chalsia one final time. He felt the sting of it, felt that old, familiar reluctance to move on. His greatest fear, he understood now, was forgetting. Without their shared bedroom, these halls, the memory of her sitting in this chair, looking into that mirror, how would he keep her alive for Tassin? For himself?

There was a scuff behind him, a shoe on the step. Embriem turned to see a young woman standing on the stoop outside. She had dark hair, a slender neck, and sad, serious eyes. Embriem didn't recognize her, but there was something about her face that was naggingly familiar.

As he turned to greet her, the girl spoke without preamble, her voice strangely flat. "I am Tilde. My father was Cockram, proprietor of the Rooster's Comb. Recently deceased."

Embriem felt a quiver of fear and had to resist the urge to reach for the door and slam it shut. Cockram was the man who'd raised a mob against him, tried to murder Marim, then set fire to the woods and the reeds. He'd been found in the forest after the fires had gone out, skull crushed by a fallen branch. Surely, his daughter was not come to finish his vendetta?

Tilde, as if reading Embriem's mind, treated him to a slow, unhappy smile. "I've come to apologize. My father was …" she paused, her eyes going misty. "My father wasn't well. For a long time, he wasn't well. His prejudices were rooted in trauma. I know that doesn't excuse what he did but I ... " She stopped again, cutting off in mid-sentence with a grimace. She held out her hand. "This was his. Before that, it belonged to my grandfather. My grandfather, a social outcast, who was said to have an unseemly fondness for brinlins."

Something in her palm glittered. Embriem, curious now, took a step forward to peer down. It was a pin, finely crafted into the shape of a golden rooster perched on a stump.

It was breathtakingly detailed, and also somehow compelling. Embriem was unable to take his eyes off it. He made himself say, "If it's an heirloom, it belongs to you."

Tilde shook her head, something fierce coming into her face. "I don't want it. I don't want ..." She stopped a third time, sighed, and ran a hand through her long, dark hair. "Please," she said. "There's power in it. He could do magic, you know, my father. Even without being bonded to a brinlin."

Unsure what else to do, Embriem held out his hand. Tilde tipped hers sideways. The glittering rooster fell into his palm. He felt a small shock when it touched his skin. She was right. This thing was alive with magic, the vessel for some ancient spell.

He looked up, prepared to ask a question, but Tilde had already turned to go. As she walked down his steps, he saw a movement at the nape of her neck. A small head peeked out at him from within the curtain of her hair.

"You're a Brinlock." He called the words after her.

She paused, looking back with a smile so tinged with sadness his heart lurched with sympathy for her. "I am my father's daughter," she agreed.

As she walked away, Embriem swung the door gently closed and walked a short distance into his entry hall, pausing under a lamp to gaze down at the small object in his hand. The pin glittered and sparkled as he held it up to the light. Its magic had a strange, sharp feel he didn't like. It reminded him of Marim's spellwork, and the weaving that had embedded its barbs into him to ride him for months.

Thinking of Marim reminded Embriem of the news he'd heard that morning. The girl intended to leave Cynnes Tarth at last, returning to Masidon with the Tessilari vessel when it sailed.

Embriem couldn't say he'd be sad to see them all go. Still, Marim had his gratitude. While she'd made mistakes, she had also saved Tassin's life twice over. That was a priceless gift.

In the entry hall, standing in the warm glow of the lamps, Embriem looked down at the pin in his palm. He would send it to Marim, he decided, with a note of thanks and farewell.

Marim walked into the bright library and blinked into the sunlight that poured into the space from above. The orb that sat at the peak of Cynnes Tarth had become translucent when repaired, and light now fell through it, uninterrupted. It sat high, high above her now, occupying the peak of the library's steep ceiling. A series of smoothed stone surfaces reflected the sunbeams, amplifying them until the entire carved out space inside the mountain seemed to glow even on dim days.

In the three months since the storm, the library had been reviewed, catalogued, and opened. Now any Brinlock in Gol Ledrith was allowed to visit this place, to read and learn of lost magics.

Coll had hardly set foot outside this place since its doors had opened. He'd always been a voracious reader, but now he worked the shelves like a man possessed. As Marim walked up to the table where he'd settled himself, he stared down at a scroll with that fevered gaze that meant he was learning, thinking, adding more knowledge to the endless depths of his mind.

He'd been cleared of any wrongdoing. When Vailria had stood before the Wheel and testified on his behalf, corroborating Marim's story that Coll alone had repaired the globe and thus untethered the storm, it was decided he'd been acting with intent to preserve the forest and the island and the Brinlocks. He'd been reprimanded for the deaths of the men in the forest and told he could undergo Keeper training if he wished to fill further defensive rolls in the woods. That was an offer he had declined, not quite as politely as Marim might have wished, and asked when he might have access to the library.

For Marim's part, she'd been thanked for her efforts and granted honorary citizenship in Gol Ledrith. Funny, she thought.

The moment she was truly welcome somewhere, she decided to leave.

Marim stood a moment next to Coll's table, waiting for him to look up. When he didn't, she pulled out the chair across from him, sat down, and flipped his book shut with a quick active push spell. He sat back, startled and annoyed. She said sharply. "You wanted to see me?"

She was annoyed as well. His message had appeared on her tablet that morning, written in his hasty scrawl. "Will you come by the library on your way to the ship?"

The request was annoying because her time was already spoken for. Marim was leaving Cynnes Tarth. She'd secured a place on the Tessilari vessel and would return to Masidon in the company of Jey and Treyam. She'd already said most of her goodbyes. Her strangest parting gift had come from Embriem. He'd sent her a vague note and a little parcel containing a swatch of fabric with a golden pin stuck through, the top carved into the shape of a rooster, and the brilliant metal containing a spark of deep, old magic. It was stowed with her other valuables now, waiting for her to have time to figure out what it was for.

Coll was not leaving – not with so many books to read. He'd been granted permission to remain in Gol Ledrith, which meant he and Marim would be parting company again. They'd known this for weeks. If he cared so much about seeing her one last time, why didn't he come to her?

Nevertheless, Marim couldn't deny his request. So she was in this strange library when she should have been enjoying a last glass of tiin and a plate of the many and varied delicacies the Brinlocks managed to create from the roots of the plentiful reeds.

Coll's annoyance cleared when he looked up and saw her. He pushed his book to the side with a smile that made her heart soften. "Marim!" He sounded excited. "I was up all night, didn't think I'd finish them both in time." He reached under the table and drew out two small, round, rocks that fit neatly in his cupped palms.

Only, they weren't rocks. As he passed one to her, Marim could feel the magic within the stone. It was a globe, not unlike the one he'd repaired on the summit of the mountain, except much, much smaller. There was a strange symbol inexpertly carved into the top. Marim touched it with her finger. "What's this?"

Coll looked up at her, his eyes both excited and vulnerable. She could remember seeing that exact same look on his face when he'd been a child, having just learned a new spell, bursting to show off. "It's my seal. Open it."

At first, Marim didn't know how. Then she saw the seam around the globe's middle. She ran her fingers over the polished surface and felt the trigger spell. She tweaked it with a thread of magic, and the top half of the globe came away in her hand.

As the halves parted, a trickle of steam drifted into the cool air of the library. Marim set the two halves back on the table.

The globe was hollow. Nestled into the arced shape of its bottom was a tiny diorama that looked a good deal like one of the basins the Brinlocks cultivated in their homes so their brinlins could exist comfortably indoors. Water lay in the bottom, and tiny reeds grew along the edge. As she stared down, uncertain, Coll began to explain in a rapid, excited string of sentences. "I started with the concept of the stitchring, obviously, but there are quite a few things about the necessary habitat brinlins must live in that make this much more challenging. Fortunately, I found help in a book." He rattled on, explaining the basic concept behind the stitchring, and how it made a portion of a single brillbane bush accessible to a single tessila. The bush itself was kept safely in a greenhouse, watered and tended by the Tessilari. Its roots were not within the spell, so the plant could be nurtured and supported without difficulty.

The challenge here was the water. Brinlins needed water, and not just any water. It needed to be the water of the warmlake, and it needed to flow. You couldn't just scoop up a basin and toss a brinlin in. The flow needed to be constant, ever cycling with the current of the lake.

He kept going, ready to explain his entire process of discovery. But Marim, who had someone else she'd promised to meet, cut him off. "Coll," she said, "this is impressive, but I'm hardly the person who most needs these. I'm Tessilari, remember?"

Coll, eyes alight with some secret delight, picked up the top half of the globe, set it back on the bottom, and worked the small latch. He set it next to the other, and pushed them both across the table towards her. Helpless to refuse him, as always, Marim picked them both up.

He sat back. His eyes were dark with lack of sleep, but he looked as pleased with himself as she'd ever seen him. His tone was a little smug as he said, "They're not for you."

Braven sat in the abandoned square near the empty fountain, watching the bustle around the Tessilari ship. Smaller vessels had come over from Lan Dinas so it could be pulled up to the quay and properly docked. Now it swarmed with activity as it took on fresh water, rations, and everything else a ship needed to make the long, perilous journey to Masidon.

At the top of the mountain, the library orb let off a soft glow. Many of the runes that had once been dead were lit now, and magic flowed through the island's heart in a gentle, uninterrupted stream. There were secrets to be unearthed in the library. The fog dial gave the Brinlocks new power over their environment. Life here on Cynnes Tarth was changing in ways most people found thrilling.

Braven's own heart, however, was heavy. The reeds along the warmlake were recovering. They had not made a full comeback overnight, as some had hoped they would, but they were replenishing themselves, day by day.

The forest was another matter. Some trees had been lost –
destroyed or killed in the blaze. More than that, though, was the
road that was to be put in, connecting Lan Dinas to Gol Ledrith.
There would still be Keepers, of course, but one of their primary
functions would be protecting travelers from the perils of the
forest. No longer would Braven be needed to preserve the danger
and mystique of the woods.

It all made Braven sad, somehow. Many spoke of rebirth, but
he could only see loss.

Sitting on a cold stone bench, Braven glanced at the sun.
Marim was late. He wondered, briefly, if she'd decided not to
come. She'd told him before how much she hated goodbyes.

His mood darkening, Braven stared at the dry fountain. If so
many things had changed, why could not Carreg Dinas be
restored? If he must lose his wood, why could he not gain a city in
its stead? Whatever repairs had been accomplished had not
extended here. The canals were still full of dust and dried weeds.
The beautiful houses were blank and stony as their empty windows
looked out over the cove.

Minutes ticked by. He was on the verge of leaving when he
heard a rustle, at last and turned to see Marim, face flushed,
hurrying towards him. "I'm sorry," she blurted the moment she
saw him. "I was delayed." Kix, who'd been flitting about on the
bright air, landed on her shoulder and hissed in his direction.

Braven felt his mood lift, as it always did at the sight of her.
Then it sank again. This was the last time they would meet, the

last time he'd watch her try to smooth her spikey hair, the last time he would receive that glare from Kix's brilliant eye.

He stood, his heart suddenly throbbing with uncomfortable pressure. "You came."

A brief look of surprise crossed Marim's face. She looked at him with her eyebrows drawn together for a moment, as if she'd just noticed something about him she'd previously overlooked. Then she seemed to shrug off whatever thought had caused her brief frown.

She took a few more steps forward, and extended her hand. At first, he thought she meant him to take it, and his heart throbbed with a dull pain. But then he saw she held something in her fingers – a small gray globe.

He let her give it to him but almost dropped it, the thrum of magic within the thing was so strong. He looked up in surprise to see her staring at him expectantly. So he explored the globe a little, found the latch, worked it, and stared down as a puff of steam drifted away on the crisp air to reveal a tiny diorama of a brinlin's pool.

His heart was hammering now, his mind scrambling frantically to catch up and find the meaning in what was happening. "I don't understand," he muttered.

She was smiling, but something else had come into her face. She drew away a little, pulling her cloak in around her body, though the sun was warm. "It's like my stitchring." Her voice had acquired a strange, neutral quality. "Only way more complicated because of the water and everything. Coll made it for you. It will let Gia come back here, to the habitat he created. It cycles its water from the warmlake and its got plenty of reeds."

Braven felt a cold claw clamp around his heart and squeeze: a rush of hope so intense it hurt.

Marim's face was pale now, and she was staring down at the ship in the harbor with an abstracted look of pain. "It means you could leave. If you wanted. It means you don't have to stay on this island forever."

He understood the subtext, and it filled him with a rush of sudden happiness. *It means you can come with me.*

Marim was still talking, her words coming out in a nervous rush. "He gave me another one, too. A spare. You'll need them both, of course, and you'll have to come back here immediately if one fails. Otherwise, the risk is too great."

For a moment, Braven closed his eyes. Down below, he could hear the crash of the waves, the shouts of the sailors. The sun was warm on his face, and there was no fog. It had been dialed back for the day to make it easier for the Tessilari ship to navigate out of the harbor. This island was his home. Could he really climb aboard a ship? Leave it behind?

When he opened his eyes, Marim was staring at him, her expression tight and fierce in a way that suggested the expectation of pain. Could she really want him to come with her? She'd never said as much.

But then, she could have given the globes to anyone.

Braven thought of that day, not so long ago, when he'd sat with Marim on the summit of Cynnes Tarth, looking at the cracked globe and sipping tiin, avoiding her questions about the magic in the mountain. He smiled ruefully. Such a curious person, he reflected, would make a good traveling companion.

He put the top back on the sphere and tucked the heavy stone into his belt pouch. With one, cautious eye on Kix, he reached out and took Marim's hand. His voice was a little tight, a little choked, as he asked, "Do you think there's room for a Brinlock in Masidon?"

Excerpt from

TESSILI ACADEMY

Chronicles of the Tessilari: Book I

A Story of Bydaira

Robin Stephen

Principal Frane and Dean Balist strode through the thriving quad. Sunlight fell on their faces, glinting off the silver threads spun into their robes. Around them, the academy was alive with life. Flowering brillbane grew along every walkway, attracting tessili to dart around the blooms like bright, delicate jewels.

Balist walked with his hands clasped behind his back, feeling pleased with his surroundings. Surely, the campus had not been so well-tended in centuries. Ever since he'd risen to his current station in Masidon and thus inherited the dean's position ten years before, he'd seen the gardens here attended to with particular devotion. And it showed.

The two men reached the murmuring central fountain. Balist paused for a moment to regard the shimmering shapes of the golden fish that shifted beneath the dancing surface of the water.

In the distance, three girls sat on one of the lawns. Their long skirts pooled around them like spilled milk. As Frane and Balist stood looking on, one of the girls said something. The other two burst into bright laughter. Balist, too far away to have heard the joke, found himself smiling along with them anyway.

Frane, at Balist's elbow, spoke. "That's the one, sir. The one in the middle. I mentioned her in my report."

Balist felt the smile leave his face. The sun, warm and pleasant a moment before, suddenly seemed overly bright. He shielded his eyes with one narrow hand. "Frane," he said, "I spoke with Nylan. He disagrees with you. He told me she's our best. An early graduation for her would be a loss for the academy. Six more months won't make such a difference."

Frane was shorter than Balist. He had the reddish hair of the people of the Fog Isles, now shot with gray. He frowned as he listened to Balist's argument. Balist knew very little about the older man, other than he'd been the principal at the academy for longer than Balist had known of its existence. The man struck Balist as overly conservative. If it had been left up to Frane when graduation occurred, the academy would have hardly any students at all by now.

Frane made no reply. He squinted towards the girls. They were smiling, their tessili flying loops around their heads. They were such sweet things, Balist thought. They sat in the sun, their cheeks smooth, hair shining, the picture of health and ease. It was the one with the blonde hair and chocolate eyes that had Frane all worked up. Over nothing, Balist was certain.

Frane said, voice grim, "It's my job, sir, to watch out."

Balist set a hand on the older man's shoulder. Frane was thin, but the wiry sinews of his arm were taut beneath Balist's fingers. "And you do your job so well. Nylan said he'll submit a full assessment after her next opportunity. We'll see what the data say. Now, come on. I'm ready for lunch."

As they turned from the girls and continued across the courtyard, the flashnodes on the walls reached full brightness. It was hard to see their progress in the sun, but now they flared to brilliance, then went out. Balist glanced over his shoulder one last time, noting how all three girls had gone still as statues. It always fascinated him, the way that worked.

For a moment, the quad was silent. The colorful tessili continued to fly, but otherwise the scene was still. For several heartbeats, it remained so. Then, one of the girls spoke. Her voice was distant, tone vague.

Balist turned away. As he waited for Frane to work the complex lock that would let them off student grounds, he felt a momentary pang of sadness for what was to come – for what always came, at the end of each year. Then, Frane swung the door aside. Balist stepped into the domed exit hall, feeling a mild relief to be out of the sun.

◆

Jey ran her fingers through Elle's long, dark hair. On the other side of the room, Kae sat at her desk, doodling with a loose ink pen as her brilliant green tessila chased the nib and nudged it this way and that, adding hiccups to what would have been smooth, flowing lines.

Outside the tall windows, the sun was dropping. The light was growing warm and rich. Soon the academy walls would throw their long shadows over the dorms.

Jey's tessila, scarlet hide brilliant in the late light, clung to the swaying sleeve of her dress. He grasped the fabric with his tiny talons as it moved with the rhythmic motion of Jey's hands.

Elle leaned back against Jey's legs, eyes closed. She hummed a vague tune while her purple tessila lay stretched out full length on her thumb, wings drooping in contented relaxation.

Jey's fingers continued their dance. Elle hummed. Jey found herself humming as well. She seemed, somehow, to know the tune.

She reached the bottom of the braid and tied it off with a golden ribbon. "What are you humming?" The room was quiet, the cloister still around them. It seemed to Jey the academy had once been crowded. Now it was silent all the time. She remembered, when she'd been young, seeing classes of six or seven girls. Now, every class seemed smaller than the last. She, Elle, and Kae were the only seniors. Younger classes had two members mostly, or sometimes just one.

"My mother used to sing that song." Elle's voice was drowsy as she spoke, but Jey felt a strange little stab. *Mother.* The word gripped her heart like an invisible claw.

Out of reflex, Jey glanced at the flashnode tucked discreetly up near the ceiling. But the light was dim, the bulb not yet a quarter full. They had time.

At her desk, Kae had stopped doodling. She turned, setting down her pen, which her tessila nudged and sent rolling across the spattered paper. Kae stopped it with an idle hand and said, in a bemused, distant voice, "Mine too."

The three of them stared at each other. Jey felt something rise up in her, some strange feeling of knowing something she did not know. She looked down, frowning. She noted the ribbon at the end of the braid she'd made was crooked. She untied it to redo the bow. As her fingers brushed the delicate contours of Elle's neck, a thought surfaced in her mind. *One hand on the throat, the other on the base of the skull. Now push.* In her mind's eye, Jey seemed to see a flash of light. She felt the memory of an exhilarating rush inside her own head. *I could kill her, just like that.*

The thought shocked her into sitting back. The ribbon fell from her fingers. The braid began to uncoil, the ends unwinding in lazy loops. Jey shot out of her chair and hurried to the counter, where the spritzer sat. She gripped the hollow crystal base and inserted the golden nozzle into her nose. She squeezed the white balloon in one hand. A mist shot out of the nozzle. She sucked it in.

Immediately, the thoughts faded. Her mind turned soft and blank. She let out a deep sigh. *It's been happening more and more lately.* But the thought had no power. It faded like a dream.

"Anyone else?" Jey said, turning back to face the room, spritzer in one hand. Elle had sat up and was completing the work of unwinding her braid. Kae's eyes had the stunned look Jey recognized too well. "Both of you," she said, setting the spritzer in Kae's hand. "Come on. And Elle, stop humming, will you?"

As Kae accepted the spritzer, Jey lifted the dangling end of her long, white sleeve. She remembered how, long ago, she had looked at the seniors and envied them their pure white dresses. Now, her tessila was brilliant against the pale folds of fabric. She raised her sleeve so he was level with her eye. She held him there for a moment. Diminutive as he was, he stared back at her with his dark, fierce eyes. Unafraid.

She heard Kae inhale, then pass the spritzer to Elle. *It takes more each week.* But again, the thought was nothing. It was as pale as a shadow in the moonlight, and meant even less.

KEEP READING
http://robinstephen.com/tessiliacademy

FREE GIFT

Thank you for reading *Brinlin Cove,* the third installment in *Annals of the Brinlocks.* If you enjoyed the book, you might like to join Robin Stephen's mailing list. You'll get some exclusive Bydaira content for free, just for signing up.

To learn more, visit robinstephen.com/free

BOOKS BY ROBIN STEPHEN

Chronicles of the Tessilari
Tessili Academy
Tessili Rogue
Tessili Revenge

Annals of the Brinlocks
Brinlin Isle
Brinlin Forest
Brinlin Cove